Ancient Blood

R. Allen Chappell

DEDICATION

Again, many sincere thanks to those Navajo friends and classmates who provided "grist for the mill." Their insight into Navajo thought and reservation life helped fuel a lifelong interest in their culture, one I had once only observed from the other side of the fence.

Table of Contents

ACKNOWLEDGMENTS

Many readers believe a book simply flows out of an author—I can assure you it does not. It requires a certain reliance on the opinions and suggestions of others, often those of a close-knit alliance of friends and family. Without these people, a writer may easily fall prey to a directionless and sometimes deadly inertia. I count myself lucky that I have such a group, and I know a great measure of the success of these little books belongs to them. And for that, I thank them.

Author's Note

In the back pages you will find a small glossary of Navajo words and terms used in the story, the spelling of which may vary somewhat depending on which "expert's" opinion is referenced.

Prologue

For nearly two thousand years the people who would later be known as the Anasazi gradually developed a culture that still astounds. Then in a matter of only a few years, totally abandoned their great pueblos and homeland, causing a disturbing yet fascinating mystery to forever shadow the canyon lands of the Southwest. It is often referred to as the "Mysterious disappearance of the Anasazi."

Over the years each succeeding generation of investigators proffered new and sometimes dissimilar theories as to the reason. It is only in the last few years irrefutable new evidence has surfaced which may satisfy all but the most recalcitrant. In the process, however, a dark and littleknown side of that ancient people is revealed. A secret long hinted at—yet often denied.

1

The Dig

Professor George Armstrong Custer bestirred himself from a drunken slumber with the full intent of carrying on business as usual; but as he gazed about the camp in a state of befuddlement, slowly came to the awareness that he was quite alone. His faithful Indian drinking companion and employee, Harley Ponyboy, was nowhere to be seen. Disconcerting as this was, equally troubling was the vague memory of a truck engine roaring to life, and then fading silently into the desert dawn. Before the realization of abandonment could take full hold, however, the professor was spared—by a shovel crashing against the side of his skull.

~~~~~~~~

　　Harley Ponyboy and George Custer had been drinking heavily for nearly three days before Harley found he could no longer keep up and enough was enough. Though still fuzzyheaded, he finally decided to risk driving the professor's big Chevy Suburban to report the matter to Charlie Yazzie. Charlie Yazzie was the one accountable in his view. It was he who set him up with the expedition— knowing full well George Custer's chancy nature. Harley was no stranger to the bottle himself and felt more than a little embarrassed at his deplorable lack of stamina. He realized too late that George Custer was in a league of his own; his Irish heritage had given him a decided advantage. Harley now felt his only recourse was to make the situation known to someone in authority before the professor should come to some harm.

~~~~~~~

Legal services investigator Charlie Yazzie was outside enjoying the morning sun and watering his new seedling peach trees when Harley Ponyboy pulled recklessly into the yard—the big Suburban sliding nearly sideways in the gravel.

Though somewhat startled, Charlie immediately recognized the vehicle and instantly feared something bad had happened. He was further convinced by Harley Ponyboy's disheveled appearance—hair sticking straight up and the left lens missing in his sunglasses. It might have been comical had it not been for the look on Harley's face.

Opening the door, Harley Ponyboy exited the truck with the exaggerated sense of propriety often seen in one who wishes to appear sober. All the way into town he had rehearsed the reasonable fashion in which he would approach the matter. He would calmly mention he felt Charlie Yazzie owned some responsibility for the state of affairs out at the dig. He meant to make it clear he himself had no part in it, other than the drinking part, of course, (that was undeniable). Instead, he just blurted out, "George Custer is drunk like a skunk. Somethin' could happen to him up there your fault, too." He abruptly caught himself halfway through this report, looked away, and leaning heavily on the door of the truck, began retching down the side of the vehicle. "It was *not* my fault," he mumbled, wiping his mouth on his sleeve. He added in a whisper, "I am only one man."

Charlie groaned and wrinkled his nose at the mess on the side of the vehicle. It took only a moment for the implications of Harley's news to sink in. "Wash up over at the hydrant Harley, then go in the house and tell Sue I said you need some coffee."

Harley Ponyboy had been off the sauce for nearly two years. He was a strong churchgoer, and Charlie had thought him nearly bulletproof in his resolve. Clearly, this was all on the head of Dr. Custer.

Charlie Yazzie had laughed when first introduced to George Armstrong Custer, certain it was a joke—but it wasn't. Dr. Custer didn't even smile. He had been through this enough times it was no longer amusing. He once enjoyed being introduced as the namesake of the infamous general, especially to Navajo, who had no dog in the fight at Little Big Horn. Now, it had grown tiresome. These days he generally just introduced himself as Dr. Custer. He had no idea why his parents had decided on George Armstrong. He suspected it was his father's idea, as *his* father had wanted *him* to be named George Armstrong Custer, a name some still thought heroic back in that time. His grandmother, however, had the good sense to oppose the move. They lived in sensitive times, she said, and felt the boy might suffer for it. Consequently, George's father was named Elmer; he swore to do better for his own son should he someday have one.

Charlie Yazzie had attended Professor Custer's classes at the University of New Mexico. He first thought to just monitor the general class on southwestern archeology, a subject he had always been keen on. He soon, however, became intrigued by Dr. Custer's thinking and signed up for succeeding classes as well.

Professor Custer—even then known as a rounder—was the object of rather pointed speculation among his peers. Many thought his theories far fetched and his personal behavior a disgrace. The man, however, did have an unsettling way of proving them all wrong. More than one detractor later became a convert, and Custer's following had become legion. The university tried to ignore his outlandish conduct, mainly due to his propensity to write rather brilliant papers—papers that brought more than a little acclaim to the university.

George Custer was now in his fifties, not a physically imposing figure but one with an undeniable charisma. Charlie Yazzie took to him at once, and Dr. Custer, in turn became impressed with the young *Dinè* and nearly convinced him to switch majors from law to archaeology. In the end, however, Charlie thought he had best keep his life directed toward the future. Having grown up on the reservation he thought he had seen enough of people living in the past.

When his old friend and mentor first called from the university, it was with the hope Charlie might ease the sometimes convoluted path to obtaining tribal dig permits. He also implored Charlie to find a dependable helper to assist in gridding the site. His graduate students would not arrive until the following week, he said. He hoped even Charlie himself might be able to squeeze in a few days of excavation at some point. He remembered how Charlie enjoyed fieldwork as a student and went so far as to promise him a look at his startling new paper, "Anasazi Migration in the End Times." He intended to publish it in the fall. "There are some dark secrets revealed in those papers," he assured in a whisper.

Harley Ponyboy had immediately come to Charlie's mind when thinking of a helper for the professor. Harley was known to be sober and reliable—and in need of a job. Charlie would have preferred to recommend old Paul T'Sosie, who had some actual hands-on experience in the business, but knew poor health was slowing him down. He might not be up to the rigors of fieldwork.

It was not that Charlie thought George Custer above his current predicament, but he thought the excitement of the new project would have kept the professor more centered. Dr. Custer seldom went off on a binge in the field, generally saving that eventuality for the boredom of academia. Charlie knew intuitively this could be the final straw for the professor—tenure or no.

Charlie Yazzie had not thought to begin his vacation tending to Harley Ponyboy and George Custer, but *he* had been the one to put that alliance together. He had thought Harley would do a workmanlike job and knew he needed the money; proof once again that no good deed goes unpunished. Sue was not going to be happy about his first day of vacation being spent rescuing drunks. She should be having the baby in the next week or so, and he was supposed to be refinishing their tiny second bedroom as a nursery. Her best friend, Lucy Tallwoman, thought it was going to be a boy. How she deduced this he couldn't say. A boy would suit him all right, but he had no real preference. Either would be all right by him.

Charlie pulled the water hose from the little peach trees and sprayed off the side of the truck. "What the hell has gotten into Professor Custer?" he wondered aloud as he turned off the water.

The sorrel gelding came to the fence and tossed his head to attract Charlie's attention. There was another horse, too, a mare, but that was Sue's horse, and it did not care for men. The mare stood back, shaking her head in a distrustful, even haughty, manner. Charlie moved to the corral, leaning on the top rail to rub his horse's jaw. He did not pat the horse. His grandfather had thought it wrong to pat a horse. "They are not dogs to be patted on the head. It disturbs their *hozo*. Rubbing their jaw is better." Later studies proved rubbing a horse's jaw does release certain endorphins that tend to calm the animal. Charlie's grandfather knew a lot about horses without knowing the why of it.

Across the highway the muddy waters of the San Juan ran deep and swift with spring melt. The she-rains, as his grandmother called them, had been good this year. His little pasture and Sue's garden were doing well for this normally parched country. He was cautiously optimistic they would not have to buy too much hay next winter. It was nearly summer and the soft breeze from the hogback ridge felt warm on the back of his neck. It carried the fresh-washed scent of cedar and sage, good medicine for a *Dinè*. The cottonwoods along the irrigation ditch already had sprouted leaves and would soon provide some respite from the coming heat of summer. This was a good little place. He and Sue had chosen wisely. Getting married last fall was the best thing that could have happened to either of them in his opinion.

When he heard the screen door slam, he looked to see Harley Ponyboy rush out of the house in a dither. "Sue's pregnant!" he announced. "You shouda' tol' me Sue was with a baby." He cocked an eye at the house. "I'da cleaned up better." He looked down at his clothing. "Now she's going to think bad about me."

Charlie chuckled. "I'll tell her it's not your fault." Guiding Harley toward the truck he continued, "And I don't think you should be driving till you feel better, either."

Harley spit on the ground and mumbled, "I'm sick a driven' anyway." Then he hauled himself up into Charlie's truck and leaned back against the headrest.

Charlie thought he knew the location of Professor Custer's dig, but once they left the highway it would be good to have Harley along to point the way. Harley didn't mind. His wife didn't expect him back for days and, in any case, he was none too eager for her to see him in his present condition.

Charlie turned to the house and saw Sue coming out with his hat and sunglasses. He shook his head in the direction of Harley and hurried up to the porch.

"Dr. Custer's on a bender," he told her simply. "I'm going to have to go up there."

"I figured," Sue frowned. "Harley pretty much told me—especially the part about how it wasn't his fault." she smiled at this and nudged her chin toward Harley waiting in the truck, now with his head out the window. "Hasn't he ever seen a pregnant woman before?" She laughed. "I thought he was going to pass out from embarrassment." She handed him his hat and sunglasses. "What are you going to do with him?"

"Take him along, I guess. I've never been to the site. It'll be easier with him along."

Sue flipped her hair out of her eyes. "Well, Lucy Tallwoman called from town and said Thomas Begay was waiting for you down at the co-op. Said you two were supposed to pick up sheetrock and trim for the baby's room."

Charlie gazed thoughtfully out across the pasture for a moment. "Yes, I hadn't forgotten. I will pick him up on the way through town and take him along, too. I may need some help up there, and Harley's not up to much right now. Plus..." He waved an arm toward the truck. "Plus...I really don't think Harley's wife should see him like this, not after all they went through last time." He had to lean over Sue's belly to kiss her goodbye. It seemed he had to lean farther each day now.

He was still feeling guilty about the sheetrock as he gunned the truck up onto the highway. He intended to get George Custer's attention when next he saw him.

~~~~~~~

Thomas Begay was leaning up against the wall of the co-op and hadn't moved more than ten feet since Lucy Tallwoman dropped him off more than an hour before.

She had a few errands to run, she said. "Then me and Sue are going 'bebie' shopping in Farmington."

Thomas grinned and called after her, "Well, don't buy too many bebies."

Lucy Tallwoman grimaced and waved a salute. "Right," she said under her breath.

Thomas wasn't one to let idle time go to waste and was having a nice little nap there against the warm wall of the feed store. He could sleep anywhere and was particularly skilled at sleeping standing up, like a horse. His black Stetson was pushed forward across his sunglasses and you would have thought he was just standing there contemplating the stacks of feed—unless you heard him snore occasionally.

When Charlie pulled up to the curb he and Harley Ponyboy looked at one another and smiled. Charlie hit the horn a good long blast. They were somewhat disappointed when Thomas calmly pushed his hat back and walked over to the truck. It took a lot to surprise Thomas. He was one of those people who didn't like surprises.

He peered in at Harley Ponyboy, who was still in a state of disarray, wearing the sunglasses with only one lens. He bumped Harley on the shoulder and pointed at the glasses. "Nice, Harley!" He lifted his Stetson and wiped his forehead on his shirtsleeve. "You and Charlie been fighting this morning?"

Harley Ponyboy stared straight ahead and said nothing. He had known Thomas a long time.

Thomas grinned, looking across at Charlie. "Change of plans?"

Charlie nodded. "Harley and George Custer have been having a little party the last couple of days up at the dig."

Harley Ponyboy turned to Thomas, "It was *not* my fault," he began, and acted as though he might say more but then didn't.

Charlie Yazzie nudged him. "Scooch over a little, Harley, so Thomas can get in." He put the truck in gear and was already rolling as Thomas slid in and slammed the door. "We're just going to check on the professor—make sure he's all right." He rubbed the back of his neck. "I wouldn't put it past General Custer to drink himself to death up there, if the hooch holds out." Charlie was clearly put out with his former professor.

Thomas leaned forward a little and looked across at Charlie. "Old man, Paul T'Sosi, was some put out with you for hiring Harley instead of him." He ignored the fact that he had to look right across Harley to say this. "I expect he'll be happy to see how that worked out."

Harley turned and pushed his face up close to Thomas, "I tol' you it was not my fault!"

Thomas held his hand up between them and wrinkled his nose. "I know, Harley. I heard you." Thomas playfully bumped Harley on the arm again, but easier this time. "Old Demon Rum gotcha, huh buddy?" Thomas said this with a touch of sadness. He knew it could just as well be him sitting there in Harley's place. He and Harley had quit drinking about the same time—over a year ago. There had been many times *he*, just as easily, might have fallen off the wagon. But Thomas had not been a member of AA like Harley. No, Thomas had quit cold turkey after the cataclysmic changes wrought by his involvement in the Patsy Greyhorse murder. Thomas Begay was a man of strong resolution, once he set his mind to a thing. He patted Harley Ponyboy on the knee and said softly, "Don't you throw up now Harley; this truck's almost new."

It had been only a few days since Thomas Begay and his father-in-law, Paul T'Sosi, had been listening to *The Navajo Hour* on KENN radio in Farmington. The old man rose before dawn and turned on his transistor radio first thing. He felt *The Navajo Hour* was one of the last vestiges of tribal culture still available to young people. He fully intended that Thomas and Lucy hear it.

The announcer was reading in Navajo from a newly released government report, loosely translating it as he saw fit. "It is estimated as high as sixty-five percent of the reservation's adult population have alcohol-related problems." His tone gave the impression he was not surprised. He went on, "A new study out today says Native Americans have a much lower tolerance for alcohol than previously thought, and a greater probability of addiction." You could nearly see the announcer smirk as he said, "I wonder how much that 'new research' cost the taxpayer?"

Thomas sighed and thought, *Maybe it isn't Harley Ponyboy's fault; maybe all Indians are victims of their genes. Or maybe Charlie Yazzie was right; maybe Indians just needed to get their shit together.*

~~~~~~~

Charlie nosed the big Chevrolet pickup north on U.S.49, just past the Colorado state line, and then hung a left on Route 160 toward Aneth, Utah. They were now only a few miles from the Four Corners Monument—where the states of Colorado, New Mexico, Utah, and Arizona join (the one place in the United States where such a phenomenon occurs). Near the turnoff to the monument someone had erected a sign that said in Navajo, God Bless America! *"Diyin God Baahózhó Nihimá Bikéyah Nízhoniye!"* Navajo are surprisingly patriotic and do not let their past differences with the U.S. government discourage their love of a country they have defended in several wars.

Once an oil and gas field mecca in the region, Aneth, had fallen upon hard times. It did, however, remain the ghostly center of a rich trove of archaeological sites involving several previous cultures. Not too far to the east, the Ute Mountain Reservation and that of the Navajo butt up against one another. That was where Professor Custer's dig was located—right in the path of the great Anasazi exodus as they fled the country over a thousand years ago. In those final years this became one of several evacuation routes for a people who had also fallen upon evil times.

Charlie pulled up to the gas pumps at the only store left in town. He figured he had enough fuel but, in this country it is considered prudent to fill up before heading into the backcountry. It is a vast land and can be an unforgiving one should one miscalculate. Harley was asleep and neither of the other two men felt it worthwhile to wake him. Charlie paid for the gas and picked up a couple of burritos for him and Thomas. He had not had time to eat the breakfast Sue had fixed him that morning and now he regretted it. She was trying out her new toaster and was having a little trouble getting the settings just right. She had quite a stack of burnt toast on the sideboard when he left but was determined to get it just right regardless of time or cost.

As far as Harley Ponyboy was concerned, Charlie doubted he could hold anything down. Not just yet anyway. Thomas, on the other hand, could eat anytime food presented itself, a particularly Indian trait passed down through millennia of hard times and not knowing where one's next meal might come from.

Charlie was beginning to get a bad feeling about George Custer.

~~~~~~

Though it was not many miles as the crow flies, the rutted track that led to the dig site was tortuous and wandering. The pitching and rolling of the truck eventually woke Harley Ponyboy, who turned a bleary eye to Thomas and whispered, "Whatcha eatin?"

Thomas quickly stuffed the last of the burrito in his mouth and mumbled, "Nothin' Harley," and licking his fingers, he swallowed and added, "Charlie don't want anyone eating in this truck."

The rough track finally ran out in a little sand wash about a quarter mile from the dig. Harley Ponyboy had pointed the way as best he could, but Charlie mostly just followed the Suburban's tracks back in.

Charlie shut down the engine and heaved a sigh of relief. "I wouldn't want to do that every day." He silently wondered how Harley Ponyboy had managed to drive out of that country, drunk, only hours before.

Harley pointed up the dirt bank to a recently pounded-out trail. "Me an' Professor Custer had ta carry everything up ta the dig," he said, rubbing the tip of his nose in thought. "Took us near half a day ta get it all up there and set camp."

"How much of it was booze?" Thomas asked, smiling.

Harley threw him a sour look and indicated with his middle finger for Thomas to get out. He and Thomas went back a long way. Back in their drinking days they had fought their way, back-to-back, out of several unpleasant situations in the Indian bars of Gallup and Farmington.

Charlie left the door open when he got out and stretched, swinging his arms to loosen up and get the feeling back. His fingers had taken a set from his grip on the steering wheel and it was a few minutes before they would straighten out.

Charlie thought it an uncommonly fine day for late spring. Distant mesas sparkled bright green in the midday sun and the warm aroma of cedar and piñon was on the breeze. Soon enough though, the diurnal winds of spring would bring sand-laden storms, and the furnace blast that sucks the life from that land leaving the low country crisp and brown.

Thomas let Harley out, then reached back in the truck, opened the glove box and looked across at Charlie. "You want me to bring the gun?"

Charlie stared at him before answering. "Do you think we'll have to shoot George Custer?"

Thomas shrugged.

Harley Ponyboy, who was now leaning into the front fender on both forearms, nodded grimly. "Shoot 'im—an' then you can shoot me too." His head was down and he was going through the motions of throwing up but apparently had nothing left to give.

Thomas Begay wagged a finger at Harley. "If you don't get better purty damn quick maybe I will shoot you— you'd be better off." Thomas made a gun of his thumb and forefinger and clicked it at Harley.

Charlie shook his head at the two and gazed off to the north where a pair of buzzards was spiraling in on a downdraft. He caught Thomas Begay's attention and with a push of his lips indicated the birds.

As they made their way up the embankment they took turns helping Harley Ponyboy, Thomas still making jokes at his old friend's expense; the two went back a long way.

When they finally straggled out on top, the three of them stood a moment taking in the camp. The tent was pitched amid a huddle of twisted piñon pines, taking advantage of the thick carpet of pine needles for bedding. A little spring trickled a silver ribbon from beneath a sandstone ledge. An errant gust of wind pushed a small dust devil through the camp, leaving a trail of fluttering papers and a snapping tent flap. As the dust cleared, Charlie could not at first see any trace of George Custer. Then, Thomas pointed to a downed cedar trunk near the tent.

Harley shook his head, holding on to Thomas for support and peering at the camp. "That's not where I left 'im." he said in a whisper. "He was pas't out in ta tent." He then confided, "I knowed I couldn't drag 'im all way ta the truck."

Thomas nodded his head sympathetically, "I doubt you coulda drug a piss ant to the truck in your shape, Harley."

Charlie left Thomas Begay to help Harley down the incline and went skittering down the slope as quickly as the loose shale would allow. Something looked wrong and fear was nipping at him as he came up to the log hiding what he assumed to be George Custer. But it wasn't George Custer; it was a bedroll with a khaki field jacket draped over it. Thomas and Harley edged up and stopped, gazing intently at the bedroll.

"That's not him," Harley managed finally, vindicated.

Thomas darted a glance his way. "We can see that, Harley."

Charlie quickly entered the tent and, after a cursory look, announced from inside, "He's not here either." After a few moments he came back carrying a small excavation shovel. It had blood with little bits of hair on the edge— hair that looked remarkably like George Custer's.

Thomas immediately turned a stern eye on Harley Ponyboy. "Harley!" he demanded, "Did you kill George Custer?"

Harley wrinkled his brow and looked long and hard at the shovel. "Well, if I did, I don' remember doin' it." He looked more closely at the implement. "That's not even my shovel. That's Dr. Custer's shovel," he said, as though to settle the question once and for all.

"Harley, we didn't think he hit himself in the head with his own shovel." Thomas shook his head and began to pick up the still fluttering papers blowing about camp.

A weak voice from the tent made them all jump. "Harley didn't do it." This was punctuated by a groan and a rustle of brush. Rushing into the tent the three Navajo saw George Custer peeking in under the back canvas. His face was covered in dried blood and the hand holding the canvas appeared twisted and swollen.

2

The Curse

When Lucy Tallwoman finally finished her errands in Shiprock, she made her way out to Sue Hanagarni-Yazzie's place. She was surprised to see Sue out in the garden, vigorously hacking away at some delinquent young tumbleweed.

"*Yaa' eh t'eeh*," Lucy called as she got out of the truck. "That is rough work for one so far along!" she said smiling. "How are you *chih keh*? Lucy used the Navajo term for "young woman" with more of a slang connotation than a reference to the difference in their ages.

Sue turned, looked up from her weeding, shaded her eyes, and waved. "I'm good." She laughed and gave a final whack with her hoe. "You've got to get these things while they are little. They'll be twice as much work later." She lay down her hoe and rubbed her hands together. "My mother said she rode a horse five miles to my aunt's *hogan* the day she had me." She raised a forearm to brush away beads of perspiration. "She said she was *ready* to have me and thought the ride might do it." Both women laughed at this. "You doing all right?" Sue asked her friend.

Lucy approached the fence nodding her head. "Good to see you Mrs. Yazzie!"

This made the former Sue Hanagarni blush. "I still can't get used to being called Sue Yazzie." She threw up her hands. "I still feel like I'm a Sue Hanagarni." The women met at the open gate and went laughing, arm in arm, to the house. Though Lucy Tallwoman was older than Sue and more traditional in the ways of the people, the two had become quite close over the past year. Each woman now considered the other her closest friend.

A lot had happened to Sue over the course of the past year and not all of it good. Her aged parents passed away— first her father and then, only months later, her mother. Neither had been well for a long while. This often seems the case with old couples that are together a very long time. It is as though they develop a symbiotic relationship over the years, each life nurturing the other until they become entwined to the extent they can no longer exist as a separate entity. They had thought themselves well past their childbearing years and were quite surprised when Sue came along. The old couple had not been well educated themselves but worked hard to see their only daughter was afforded the best possible opportunity in that regard. Sue's good job at legal services and marriage to law school graduate Charlie Yazzie seemed to them to be ample compensation. They had at least lasted long enough to see their only daughter married and happy, and that had made *them* happy. They thought they had then come full circle and done their part to bring *hozoji* to the people.

Charlie's grandmother had also passed away that winter leaving him and Sue without any close relatives. Charlie still had more distant relatives but was drifting yet farther away from the more traditional life close family might encourage.

Sue was on maternity leave from Legal Services and was learning to care for her first home and getting to know her new husband. If things worked out as they hoped she thought to take several months off and stay home with the new baby. She suspected they might not be able to afford such a luxury, but it was something to think about.

She and Charlie had not wanted to make a big deal of the wedding. They knew Sue's parents would want to contribute to the cost, something the old couple could ill afford. Also Sue felt what money *they* had saved would be better spent on their little place outside town. After the justice of the peace had married them, there was a small family gathering with only Sue's parents, Thomas and Lucy with their two children, and Lucy's father, Paul T'Sosi, in attendance. Paul sprinkled the newlyweds with blue corn pollen and offered up a wisp of sacred corn meal to both earth and sky. He did this while singing a chant ending with the words of the Beauty Way.

Traditionally, Navajo marriages are simple affairs with little ceremony. Generally the new husband just moves in with the woman's family and they begin their new life from there. At the time of *her* wedding, Sue suspected Paul might be inventing some of their particular ceremony. But he was well versed in Navajo culture and she knew he would do his best for them. Sue thought, *Maybe his years working at the Episcopal mission had made him feel there should be more to it for a couple starting a new life together,.* In any case, it was done and she had never been happier.

When she became pregnant, Charlie said, "After this baby is born we'll put together a real celebration—maybe have Paul T'Sosi do a full Blessing Way."

Sue looked at him. "Are you sure a 'Blessing Way' would be the thing?" she asked.

Charlie only shrugged and said, "We'll see."

At the kitchen table Sue and Lucy sat over cups of coffee and talked about "bebies". The Navajo word for baby is *Ah-wayh*. Sue thought it a funny word and suspected it might have come about because babies make that sound when they cry: "Ah-whaa Ah-whaa."

Sue remembered reading somewhere that less than half the people on the reservation still spoke fluent Navajo— most of those who did were older and isolated in a more rural lifestyle. There were even a few people left who spoke relatively little English. Sue, though coming from older and more traditional parents, did not speak Navajo as well as they had, and even that was beginning to slip away. There was, of late, a quiet resurgence afoot on the reservation designed to promote a greater understanding of Navajo culture, including the language. While some young people professed an interest in this movement, most were more interested in the same things young people everywhere are occupied with; television and music. Though Sue had long been attuned to life in the white world, she still was amazed at the grasp of English and slang she heard from the younger crowd. *Life goes on,* she thought *Life on the reservation changes...and yet, it remains the same.*

Sue did believe her husband had grown more comfortable with his Navajo roots. Still, his long years away at school left him somewhat at a distance from the more traditional side of the culture. His grandmother had been his last real tie to the old ways. He still had his great-aunt Annie Eagletree, but while old, even she was entranced by television—cop shows mostly. On her occasional visits, Aunt Annie often spent a good bit of time explaining to Charlie the latest investigative techniques. She often inquired if he had been practicing with the .38 Chief's Special the family had given him as a graduation present.

Some of the family had thought the words. "Chief's Special" on the Smith & Wesson box meant it was suitable for a Chief. When questioned, the gun salesman assured them this was probably the case (he had sold a lot of Chief's Specials this way and was prone to be agreeable on the subject). In the gun store that day Annie Eagletree kept quiet, as she did not want to appear rude. Once outside, however, she confided to everyone it really meant *Police Chief's Special.* When he heard this, Annie's husband, Clyde, who'd had a few drinks earlier, wanted to go back in the store and kick the store-man's ass. Fortunately the family was able to convince Clyde he was too old to kick anyone's ass, especially a white gun-store owner who probably wouldn't tolerate it.

As Sue refilled their coffee cups she told Lucy about Harley Ponyboy coming in drunk that morning and mentioned that Charlie, Thomas, and Harley had all gone back up to George Custer's camp to check on him. "They may not make it back tonight. If they do, Charlie will probably drop the other guys off. He'll be going right by both places on the way back." She chuckled. "What's up with Harley? She twirled a strand of her hair and turned more serious. "He nearly went to pieces when he saw I was pregnant." She stirred her coffee. "That Harley's a funny guy I think."

Lucy added more sugar to her cup and was silent a long moment. "We have been knowin' Harley a long time." She brushed an imaginary crumb from the table and went on, "Thomas says Harley is a big believer in *Yeenaaldiooshii*—witches—and that stuff." Lucy fidgeted in her chair. "A long time ago, when Harley and Anita were first married, Harley got crosswise with a very bad person over around Ganado. Some said that person was a witch." Lucy lowered her voice and peered about the room as though someone might be listening. "That man knew Harley had just gotten married and he put a curse on Harley. He told Harley he would never have children. He said anytime Harley even touched a pregnant woman she would lose her baby." Lucy looked out the kitchen window and grew quiet for a moment. "Anita lost two babies before they quit trying. They never had any more children."

A cold shiver ran down Sue's back, and she had to shake herself to throw it off. "Well, he never touched me! Wouldn't even look at me after he saw I was pregnant. You don't think…?"

Lucy bit her lip and looked down at her cup. "I will talk to my father. He will know what to do." She caught herself, brightened, and forced a smile. "That is, if anything needs to be done at all."

~~~~~~~

Aida Winters paused in her digging to watch her two young charges at work in the flower garden—just as their mother had once worked there beside her. They were squabbling back and forth, as siblings will do and Aida kept a curious ear to their conversation. Ida Marie Begay was now eight years old and already had caught up with her classmates at school. She'd had no schooling before her father gained custody after their mother's death the previous year. Ida Marie's brother was seven and would be ready for second grade next fall. They were bright children and had taken to their new life with an exuberance that surprised even their father.

Being adaptable has always been the Navajo strong suit—they seem to embrace change better, perhaps, than any other indigenous people in the Southwest. This is thought to be a major contributing factor to the steady increase in their numbers over the last century. They are one of the few tribes to do so and are now the largest single tribe in the United States.

The two children were vigorously debating which flowers would look best on their mother's grave. These children did not have the traditional Navajo superstitious fear of the dead. Aida thought this a blessing and hoped they would not fall under that influence later on. She could barely believe it was only a year since their mother, Sally Klee, had been shot to death, right there on Aida's front porch. She allowed herself a grim smile of satisfaction. Everyone involved in Sally's death was now dead themselves or in prison, which was probably a worse fate for an Indian.

"Ida Marie Begay!" she called sharply, "Let your brother have a say in those flowers!" Aida always called her Ida Marie. Sally Klee had given her daughter Aida's middle name, 'Marie' in deference to the years of help and love Aida lavished on her growing up. She would probably have given her Aida's first name as well had her adoptive Ute family been on better terms with her. Still, Aida savored the name each time it was spoken. Neighbors thought it strange that a white woman, and one of some means at that, would take two Indian children as her heirs. They didn't understand. This child's name and her memories of Aida would one day be all that was left of Aida Marie Winters. She had no one beyond these two children. The boy, Caleb Thomas Begay, was bright and engaging and was showing the inherent charm and beguiling nature of his father. Aida smiled and thought, *the boy would bear watching on that account.*

Thomas Begay had been good enough to let the children come visit for a part of their summer vacation. His father-in-law, old Paul T'Sosi, thought they might be better off under *his* tutelage rather than that of a white woman rancher and horse trader. Secretly, however, he knew there were often advantages to be gained from associating with whites. He had learned a good bit from white people himself. He thought, *herding sheep and listening to an old man prattle on about old ways might not carry them as far in today's world.*

In the little cemetery on the hill behind the house, Aida and the children were debating the placement of their flower arrangements.

"Well, I think these roses would look better in front," Ida Marie asserted with a cross look at her brother.

Her brother scowled and replied, "Just 'cause *you* think so don't make it so!"

Aida was about to quash the argument when she happened to look up and see a smudge of dust far up the road leading to the ranch. The mailman and his little white jeep did not stir up so much dust. It was someone else and they were in a hurry. She shaded her eyes with a hand and wondered who could be calling so late in the day. She stooped to help the children place the flowers and then hurried them down the hill toward the house.

They had almost reached the yard when Charlie's white truck slowed and pulled into the drive. Aida frowned. *Now what?* She could see Thomas leaning out the window and waving. Surely he was not back for the children so soon—she was supposed to have them for three weeks at the least.

As the truck rolled to a stop, Aida could see four men inside and was somewhat alarmed when Thomas and Charlie helped an obviously injured white man out of the vehicle. A third Navajo stood looking on, occasionally wringing his hands—he had only one lens in his sunglasses.

Charlie spoke first, "Hi, Aida, good to see you again," and without further ado launched into the reason for them being there, "We've run into a little problem down-country and thought you might be able to give us a hand."

She could now see the white man was badly hurt and hurried to clear the way to the house and hold the door for them. "Put him there on the sofa," she said.

The children held back, uncertain at the strange doings, but smiled at Thomas Begay when he threw them a sidelong grin.

George Custer lay back with a sigh and held his injured hand on his chest to avoid dirtying the couch. Charlie had cleaned him up as best he could, but the facilities had been meager. George, his eyes nearly swollen shut, was embarrassed and smiled weakly in the direction of Aida's voice. She, in turn, regarded him in a much more thoughtful and calculating manner.

"This man needs to go to the hospital," Aida announced, moving toward the kitchen. "What possessed you to bring him here?"

Charlie followed her out of the room, and as she ran water in a basin, he attempted to explain, "Aida," he searched for just the right words, "we had nowhere else to turn. George refused to be taken to a hospital or even let us call in tribal police for help." He picked up the pan of water from the sink. "I just thought…if word gets out it could be the end of his career."

"What sort of trouble is he in?" Aida was getting over her surprise. "He stinks of whiskey but I expect there's more to it than that."

"His name is George Custer, and he's an archaeology professor from the University of New Mexico—"

"I know who he is!" Aida interrupted. She turned with a sharp look. "I *know* who he is." she was trembling slightly now. "What I can't figure out is why he would have you bring him here."

Now it was Charlie's turn to be surprised. "Uh…he didn't have us bring him here. Thomas thought of it." He narrowed his eyes. "You know George Custer?"

She was at the linen closet then and brought forth a stack of cotton dishtowels, worn thin but soft and bleached clean. "Get my vet kit by the back door," she said and, taking the container of water from him, she returned to the living room.

When Charlie came back with the medical supplies, the gash on the side of George's head had already been cleaned. He could see now it was not as bad as it first appeared. Aida proceeded to irrigate the injury with saline solution from the kit. "How long's he been like this?"

"You mean drunk…or cut?" Thomas queried, not sure what she was getting at. "He's been drunk about three days, according to Harley." He looked over at Charlie. "We're not sure how long it's been since he got hit in the head."

"One of your guys do it?" Aida asked, digging through her folder of suture packets.

Thomas frowned. "Harley helped him get drunk, but swears he didn't hit him in the head." He smiled engagingly. "Charlie and me is just the rescue party."

Aida examined the cut more closely. "Another few hours and the edges would have dried out. I'd of had to trim them back before putting in stitches; that would've hurt." She glanced up at Charlie. "Good thing I put a coverlet on this couch when the kids came; they like to eat while they're watching cartoons. Otherwise you boys would owe me a couch."

Charlie and Thomas looked uncomfortable. Thomas had not long ago finished paying Aida for the horse he bought from her the previous fall. This was good news about the couch; he was not eager to incur further debt with this woman.

"You think he'll need a little deadener?" Aida looked up at them. "I've got some Xylocaine here I use on the horses when I have to stitch one up."

"Naaa," Thomas ventured, "I think he's plenty deadened already." Thomas himself had been sewn up several times when drunk and not always by doctors, either. "I expect he's got enough painkiller in him already."

Charlie winced but suspected Aida had put many a stitch in man and beast, and he was fairly confident the job would be done to the best of her ability. It was the rare rancher in that country who couldn't put in a stitch or two when required.

Harley Ponyboy was finally sobering up and had been pacing nervously up and down the front porch, occasionally peering in through the screen door. He warned Ida and Caleb to stay outside with him. The children were now sitting on the porch swing, and Harley gave it a little push as he passed by. The children had grown solemn, and while they knew Harley, they had not seen him in such a state before. They thought it best to do as he said. They saw Harley as the old kind of people. Who knew what those people might do should the mood strike them. Their new grandfather, Paul T'Sosi, was the old kind of Navajo, too, but he liked kids; Harley didn't seem to.

George Custer was coming around rather well by the time the procedure was finished, and while he had yelped a couple of times, he had acquitted himself quite well, in Thomas's view. The men did have to hold his hands away from his face a time or two, but only now and again. His mangled hand received an examination as well, and Aida thought there might be some small bones broken. There was nothing for it now, however, but to clean and bandage.

When George was finally tended to and sleeping, the others gathered on the front porch. Thomas went to sit with his kids on the swing and whispered in their ears. He must have said something silly, as Caleb giggled and Ida Marie looked up and smiled. It had only been a few days since he dropped them off at Aida's, but they were happy to see him, just the same.

Charlie, sitting on the front steps, spoke finally and said they had better get George Custer back in the truck and down to his and Sue's place, as he knew of nowhere else to take him. "George's students will be up from Albuquerque next week to get started on the dig. George has to be ready for that, or suffer the consequences."

Thomas looked at Aida. He knew Charlie didn't have room for the professor at his place and neither did he. Unless, of course, Dr. Custer wanted to sleep under the stars in the "summer *hogan*" and undergo the third degree from Paul T'Sosi about why he had hired Harley Ponyboy instead of him.

Aida seemed suddenly tired and leaned against a post. "You boys might as well leave him here for a few days, I guess," she frowned, "Jouncing around in that truck isn't going to do him any good." She looked pointedly at Harley Ponyboy. "Hell, he might even have a concussion."

Harley raised a finger and started to say something, then thought better of it and remained silent.

Aida brushed the back of her hand across her mouth and looked out across the yard. "He and I have a few things to talk over, anyway."

Thomas looked sharply at Charlie but remained silent.

"You sure having George *and* the kids won't be too much?" Charlie asked.

"No, these kids are no trouble, and they'll be a big help once I get 'em lined out." She looked over at the children and smiled. "Those two make me laugh," she said and then turned back to Charlie. "I had almost gotten out of the habit."

~~~~~~~~

Old Paul T'Sosi was out of sorts. He had not slept well and had dreamed of his mother and Magpie and Coyote. He did not often dream of the dead, and the very thought of it preyed on his mind. As far as the two tricksters—Magpie and Coyote—he tried never to think of them at all. It was a bad omen, he was sure. He recalled Magpie, who was a great talker and the smarter of the two, commenting on Paul's lack of attention to the deities here of late. The bird had gone so far as to say no good could come of it. Coyote kept his own council but silently nodded in what might have been agreement. It was worrisome to see these two pranksters together and in accord. It was generally Magpie that bedeviled Coyote and while it was common to see them together at, say, a winterkill, they were generally not on good terms. The Navajo had long ago learned to pay heed to the doings of these two beguilers.

Paul had fallen in and out of health over the last few months and it had taken a toll on his hozo and on the hozo of those around him as well. The old man was not one to tread lightly when in a bad mood. It still rankled that Charlie had not recommended him for George Custer's archaeology expedition. Charlie was well aware he had participated in major excavations in the past and had indeed assisted several well-known archaeologists. *That Harley Ponyboy knew nothing about being an archaeologist's assistant.*

He called up the dog and went to turn out the sheep. The dog stood anxiously watching the little band file from the corral. He thought it odd to be taking them out so late in the day. Paul's daughter, Lucy Tallwoman, had admonished him to let the sheep be and stay inside and rest. She said she would bring a couple of bales of hay from town when she came back that evening. He had waited the better part of the day. *Those sheep had lambs; they could not go the entire day without some sort of feed. Ewes couldn't make milk from thin air. Even just a couple of hours grazing would settle their nerves and bring the milk.*

Once again the sheep would have to depend on an old man who would have been better left abed. If Thomas had not been off gallivanting with Charlie, *he* could have taken the sheep out today. Paul understood that Thomas needed the work, and Charlie was very fair with him in that regard. Still there were the sheep to consider; always there were the sheep. Where would the family be without these old-line Churros and their long stringy wool, which weaves like no other? Lucy's reputation had grown to the point that there was a waiting list for her blankets, and collectors were scrambling to outbid one another. He had never seen the likes of it. Her mother had been a noted weaver as well, but *her* weaving had never commanded the prices now set by Lucy's work. The major portion of the family's income came from Lucy's weaving of this very wool. Without it things might be quite different indeed. He thought to himself, *That was the way young people were these days—*

always thinking of fun and running around, when there was
plenty to do right there at home.

He figured he would take the sheep to the sage flats
across the highway, just for an hour or so. They had not
been over there for more than a month, and the spring rains
should have some new grass cropping up.

It was not so cold, but there was a sharp little breeze
from the upper ridges. He wore the new earmuffs he had
been given for Christmas. He thought it best he get some
use out of them before his new grandson wore them out.
The earmuffs were made of rabbit fur, and young Caleb
Begay loved to sneak them away and wear them when the
old man wasn't looking. Paul T'Sosi smiled when he
thought of it. That boy was like his own grandson now—a
grandson he would otherwise never have. He would get the
boy a set of earmuffs just like these the next time he was in
town. With summer coming on, Caleb wouldn't get much
use from them, perhaps, but they would keep him from
putting Paul's earmuffs on the dog or whatever lambs he
could catch. That boy was getting more like Thomas every
day.

The sheep hesitated a moment at the black ribbon of
asphalt, just as they always did, but the dog nipped and
threatened until the leaders gave in and began crossing. The
old man spared only a glance each way before following
and saw nothing. As the dog pushed the little band across
the road, a lamb just beside Paul lost it's footing on the
smooth asphalt and went down. Paul stooped to right the
little fellow before it got trampled and did not hear the
stock truck until the screech of its tires penetrated his
earmuffs. The truck's driver, momentarily distracted while
tuning his radio, had come around the bend unaware—and
much too fast. When he did look up, he swerved the truck
and applied the brakes at the same time, locking the wheels
and skidding sideways through the last of the sheep—and
Paul T'Sosi.

The old man lay crumpled in the barrow ditch along with two ewes and the lamb he had tried to help. Six other sheep lay strewn across the road in pools of blood and gore, the bowels of one stretching from one side of the road to the other. The goats, more clever than sheep, stayed at the front of the flock and sustained no casualties. In the wild it is generally the stragglers that are most in danger. Of all domestic animals sheep are one of the few who can no longer survive on their own in the wild. Goats, on the other hand, are famously independent of man and do quite well on their own regardless of where they might be cast out.

Paul T'Sosi felt only a quiet pleasantness, certainly not pain, as Magpie and Coyote came by and stopped at the edge of the road to have a look. They appeared to be speaking to one another as they watched but he couldn't quite make out what they were saying. *It must be the earmuffs*, he thought lazily, and then again dreamed of his mother.

~~~~~~~

As Charlie topped the rise, just before the turnoff to Lucy Tallwoman's camp, Thomas grabbed the dash with both hands and opened his mouth but made no sound. The whirling red lights of the tribal police cars cast an ethereal glow over the cleanup operations in progress. The dog still held the remainder of the little band of sheep and goats in a tight knot on the far side of the highway. This was not easy to do, as goats pay less attention to a dog than do sheep and the goats wanted to go home. But it was what the dog was bred to do, and he intended to do it as best he could.

"Looks like your sheep got loose!" Charlie exclaimed pulling to the side of the road.

"No, they didn't get loose," Thomas whispered while reaching for the door handle. One of the tribal boys was already on his way over and met Charlie halfway while Thomas stood quietly surveying the carnage.

It was Hastiin Klah. He had been a policeman for a long time and knew his business when it came to this sort of thing. "Do you know whose sheep these are," he asked Charlie, noting his official truck.

Charlie indicated Thomas, who heard the question but didn't bother turning to the policeman. He and Hastiin Klah had done business before "They are my wife's sheep," Thomas said over his shoulder. "Where is the old man?" He stared silently at the earmuffs on the edge of the road.

"The ambulance took him away. Farmington, I guess. He looked in pretty bad shape." He waved a hand in the direction of the other officer. "We're just giving the highway boys a hand getting this mess cleaned up."

~~~~~~~

Old Paul T'Sosi was dreaming again. This time his mother appeared closer and was as young and lithe as when he was a boy. She had been a great runner in her youth and fearless in the defense of her flocks. Now each time Magpie and Coyote came close, she would charge at them, shoo them away and then beckon him to follow her into the light of dawn—at least it looked like the dawn, with bands of luminescence swirling all around her. He had nearly decided to go with her, when a sharp jab caused him to change his mind. He was just too tired. It was as though he was being physically pulled away from the light and drawn back into darkness.

The doctor taped the needle in place and stood back looking thoughtfully at the old man. He had been a doctor in this country for over twenty years and had attended hundreds of injured Indians, yet it never ceased to amaze him how tough and tenacious of life they were. Things that might kill a white person outright were often just a bump in the road for these people. Many thousands of years of natural selection had made them so. He wondered how long they would retain this ability in their relatively new life in the soft modern world.

Paul came at last to an uneasy awareness. Now there was pain, not in any particular place or intensity, but all over. His entire body ached, and he could hear nothing above the roar of his own blood coursing through his veins. Eventually, however, his mind began to find order and then cleared enough to allow the processing of a few thoughts, the first of which was where he might be. He guessed a hospital.

The passing of his wife several years back had made him familiar with the sounds and smells of such a place, and he now decided this was indeed where he was. There was a sense of urgency all about him, but in a calm, directed manner that bespoke healers going about a task they were intimately familiar with. These were not his kind of healers. Their magic was of a different sort and, while it might work well for their kind, he was not so sure it would work for him. It had not worked for his wife—but then, neither had his.

He had lain quite still for some time. In fact, he was not sure he could move at all. It had grown quiet. His first thought was to try to open just one eye. That would tell him if there was some glimmer of hope. In his experience as a healer, hope itself was a powerful medicine. Even a tiny bit of it often went a long way. He cracked one eyelid slightly, and that went well. There was light, sunlight, he thought, and he felt the ultraviolet warmth of it on his hand at his side. This was all to the good, and he opened both eyes. The first blurry image he saw was his daughter, Lucy Tallwoman, sitting beside his bed and looking directly at him.

"*Ah-hah-lah'nih*," she said softly, tilting her head slightly and smiling. "You have been in another place for a while now. I was afraid you might not come back from that place." She reached and took his hand. "The doctor said you was a tough old bird." She smiled and moved to the side of the bed.

At first the old man had to think about how to make the words but finally said in a low, raspy voice, "How are those sheep?"

"It could have been worse. We lost nine head of ewes and a lamb, but two of those ewes were old and didn't lamb this year anyway. A couple of others are limping around but they will get over it." She squeezed his hand. "We still have twenty-three ewes, eight goats, and the ram. The cop said he didn't have to put any down—either they were dead, or they were okay. It was Hastiin Klah. He happened by right after the accident. He was just getting off duty and on his way home."

"Well, that was lucky, I think," Paul said softly.

Lucy nodded her head. "Thomas and the boys got there just after the ambulance took you away. They said the dog had the sheep off the road and held them until he and Harley could get them back up to the corral. Charlie called the dispatcher, and she left a message at Sue's house. I came straight here."

"Harley Ponyboy? I thought he was with George Custer?"

Lucy ignored the question, straightened his pillow and gave him a sip of water from the glass on the tray. "Thomas was here until just a few minutes ago. He left to feed the sheep. I had the hay in the truck already." She said this last to let her father know she had not forgotten to get hay.

"Oh," Lucy said, "I had the usual hassle at the front desk about your name on the paperwork. They didn't want to believe you spell your name T'Sosi instead of T'sosi." She laughed. "Do you know how many times I have had to explain that to white people who think everyone should spell their name the same as everyone else with that name?" She frowned. "That's one reason I go by Lucy Tallwoman. Well, that and the rug buyer saying I would sell better with a name white people thought was more Indian."

Old Paul T'Sosi sat straight up in bed at this, gaining strength from indignation. "Well, I hope you told her why we spell it that way. Most Navajo names are spelled as they are because that is how some white person first spelled them." The old man grew more animated and declared, "It's T'Sosi! These people need to learn the right way to say it. You have to touch your tongue to your teeth and spit the whole thing out at once. The *S* is just as important as the *T*. That's the way your grandfather spelled it, and that's the way I'm going to spell it too."

"I know, Dad, I told them. I said, 'Just because everyone else on the reservation spells it the other way, don't mean we have to.'" She smiled and patted his hand.

"And," the old man said, "your Navajo name *is* Tallwoman—*Asdzaa Nez* in Navajo. Your grandmother gave you that name. She said she had never seen so long a baby and called you *A'teed Nez* (Tall Girl) and later when you grew up it became *Asdzaa Nez*. Your Navajo name is what makes you strong." The old man looked at his daughter. "I named you Lucy, after a little girl in a comic book. She was a bossy little girl, and I thought that suited you."

3

The Cure

The morning after George Custer's impromptu arrival, Aida rose early to set the kettle and start breakfast. She liked to get a head start on the children and was prone to let them sleep in. She was afraid she might be spoiling the pair but had little previous experience to go by. Indians are known for indulging their children, and as far as she knew, no real harm seemed to come of it. She put on a pot of oatmeal and was about to check in on George Custer, when she turned to find him standing in the doorway. "How's the head?" she asked briskly, gathering cups from the cabinet and moving to the table without looking directly at him.

"Better." George's face was not nearly so swollen now, though he still peered at Aida through slitted eyes and with a quizzical half-smile. "What has it been now, Aida—ten years?"

"More like twelve, I guess—but who's counting," she went on setting the table, then paused a moment and noted, "Time passes more quickly for some than others, I suppose."

George Custer nodded, then looked suddenly pale and leaned heavily against the doorjamb. He took a moment to collect himself and then said, "I wrote several times from Guatemala. I never heard anything back. The mail's unreliable at best down there."

"I got the letters. I burned them. Didn't read a one."

George only nodded again and looked down. *Maybe that had been for the best. She was right to burn those letters. It had been a silly thing for me to do after so long a silence. But it was not like I could just walk down to the post office. I should have just let it lie.*

"I meant to come down and see you as soon as the undergrads had things underway up at the Aneth site." This was not strictly true, and while the thought *had* crossed his mind, he'd had no real intention of calling Aida Winters. That bridge had been burned and the years had rendered the break irreparable to his way of thinking. Yet, there remained that niggling little doubt that often assails the most resolute of decisions.

"I'm sure you had the best of intentions," she said dryly as she brought two mugs, then hesitated, "You still drink tea I assume?"

George nodded and moved to the chair opposite Aida. "Yes, we still have that in common, at least."

Aida stopped mid-pour and contemplated the man before her, beaten down and rough, as he now appeared. She recalled a good deal they once had in common in the year after her husband's passing. At the time, she had thought it fortuitous that her ranch harbored eight verified Anasazi sites, ranging from smaller pre-Pueblo to a well-preserved complex of an era commonly referred to as the Golden Age of the Anasazi.

Nearly every ranch around boasted at least one or two sites, some long plowed under, of course, but still they were there under the furrows. Aida's ranch was different—from the earliest of the family owners, little digging had been allowed. There were the usual potholes, of course, made mostly by locals sneaking in back in the day when train-car loads of artifacts were being shipped east, even to foreign collectors and museums. It had been an easy way to pick up badly needed dollars for settlers in a harsh land where cash was hard to come by. But for the most part, Aida's ruins lay nearly pristine in their hidden side canyons.

George spooned in a half-measure of sugar and stirred his tea, clicking the side of the spoon against the cup before taking a delicate slurp. "Did the university ever contact you about excavating the main site?"

"They did, on your recommendation I believe." She said this with only a hint of disdain. "I told them no and didn't hear from them again."

"Probably just as well," George murmured. He paused, and then went on, "There have actually been great strides in the science just these last few years." He became more animated. "Why, do you know, they can now recover viable DNA that's traceable to people still living today and to other lines of similar people in other areas?" The old excitement was on him then, and Aida almost smiled at the glimpse of the old George Custer peeking through.

Aida's husband had originally contacted the university in regard to surveying the ruins, thinking there might be some future value in knowing exactly where the sites fit in the Anasazi occupation of the area. Several local ranches had sold for prices far beyond their agricultural valuation due mainly to similar archeological sites. He believed they might help the ranch provide a nice little cushion for Aida should something someday happen to him, a belief that proved prophetic as he was taken by a stroke only months later.

UNM is not known for its lightning decisions when it comes to archeological allocations. Aida's husband had already been gone nearly a year when George Custer finally pulled into the yard in his shiny, new university vehicle and stylish clothes. The man fairly reeked of academia and the excitement of distant lands. His charm and glib Irish tongue had a power to it, and Aida was swept away, though she was not ordinarily one to be swayed by such things. Now, looking back, she was inclined to believe it was the void left by her husband's passing that allowed such vulnerability to the professor's dashing persona.

George Custer, for his part, found the widow a refreshing change from the sort of women he had previously known—and there had been many. Aida's take-charge attitude and forthright demeanor captivated him from the start. And he thought her not bad looking, in a wholesome sort of way. It also had not hurt that George had instantly taken a fatherly interest in the little Ute neighbor girl, Sally Klee, who had recently attached herself to Aida. The girl found her neighbor to be an island of calm and a welcome escape from the chaotic life of her Ute relatives. The notorious Buck clan had been Aida's neighbors and nemesis all her life, and she was well aware of their treatment of Sally. The child had quickly become fascinated with the professor, a man unlike any she had known. He could speak a smattering of both Ute and Navajo and could tell stories from both cultures, and others from lands far away. Years later, when grown and living with Thomas Begay, Sally Klee would recount for him those tales and fondly recall the professor who had been a brief part of her childhood. Perhaps that was what caused Thomas to suggest Aida's place as a refuge for the injured archeologist these many years later. When questioned, however, Thomas claimed he had no real recollection of anything that might have prompted the suggestion.

George Custer had managed to drag out the archeological survey of Aida's ranch for nearly the entire summer back then, inventing reasons for the additional exploratory excavations he deemed necessary to verify this or that minor supposition.

In the end, however, a previously applied-for grant involving a much more important project in Guatemala, came to fruition—an opportunity the professor had long coveted. He could delay no longer.

While Aida was devastated at the news, she tried to understand and hoped they could maintain an ongoing relationship during what she hoped would be a short absence. She was naturally sick at heart but waited hopefully—nearly three long months—for some word from Central America.

Aida Winters was not a woman easily taken advantage of, nor would she suffer it lightly. By the time a letter did eventually arrive, she had formed a new and hardened resolve in the matter of George Custer. She burned his letter without opening it, an action affording her but little satisfaction. She burned the ensuing few letters as well, some looking as though they had come a portion of the distance by pack mule, which in fact, they had. It was a measure of the woman's character that she allowed herself no feelings of remorse. Never again, she thought, would she let herself be taken in by a man like George Armstrong Custer.

"Oatmeal?" she asked, arranging bowls on the table.

"That would be fine," George replied. "I like oatmeal."

"I know," Aida murmured as she busied herself at the stove. She could not help but wonder what twisted fate had brought George Custer once again to her door.

~~~~~~~~

Charlie held the sheetrock in place while Thomas Begay nailed it to the studs in the nursery wall. Harley Ponyboy was huffing and puffing as he ferried supplies and tools back and forth from the truck and then began mixing a batch of spackling mud. Harley had volunteered to help out on the project, as he had nothing better to do now that activities were suspended at the dig. Charlie felt obligated in a way and paid him a bit, but not as much as Thomas, who was the only one of them who actually knew what he was doing. The work was going quite well in his opinion and everything should be in place by the time the baby came, assuming Sue could hold off three or four more days. Sue and Harley avoided each other as best they could, though Charlie had made light of the supposed *curse* afflicting Harley Ponyboy.

"That is how these things always get started," Charlie stated emphatically. "Someone comes up with a *curse* to put on another person, and that person obsesses on it until he finds some little thing to support it, and it grows from there. In the meantime, the one who laid the *curse* is elevated to *Witch* in everyone's eyes and his reputation grows! It's just silliness!" Charlie, who had been eating a piece of burnt toast with jam, shook his finger at no one in particular, brushed a few crumbs from the front of his shirt and looked at his plate. "How much of this toast do we have left now?" He frowned when Sue didn't answer. "It is all silliness. The only power in those *curses* is people's misplaced belief in them."

"What about Anita losing her first two babies then?" Sue challenged. "What was that all about?"

Charlie gave an exasperated sigh. "I don't know...coincidence, maybe...or an unknown medical condition. It could have been any number of things, but I guarantee you it wasn't any damned *curse*," he said, inadvertently cursing in the process and raising his voice at the same time—things he did not ordinarily do.

Sue made a face behind his back. "You know I'm not big on this stuff myself." Sue raised her own voice, "I'm just saying... that's all. I'm just saying." Her voice trailed off as she watched Charlie stomp out the back door.

Two days later, the nursery was finished, but still Sue showed no immediate sign of coming up with a baby for it. She was now past the time the health service doctor had proposed for the new arrival. She became antsier and a bit more cross as the days passed. Finally, she decided to go visit Paul T'Sosi, who was to be discharged from the hospital that very afternoon. She had not been to see the old man as yet, and if she waited till later, it would mean a much longer drive out to Lucy Tallwoman's place.

At the hospital, Sue arrived just as visiting hours commenced (the hospital was quite strict in that regard, and many a relative, even those who had traveled long distances, had suffered because of it). Paul was sitting up in bed and, with the prospect of release drawing near, was looking quite chipper. He was a little surprised to see his daughter's friend Sue—and alone too.

"Sitsi! It is good to see you, and good of you to come see an old man." He self-consciously arranged the bed coverings about him and ran a wrinkled hand through his hair. He sounded concerned when he asked, "Should you be out driving that old truck this close to your time?"

Sue smiled. "Oh, it's fine. This baby apparently intends to give us plenty of time to get ready, which is a good thing, as it turns out." She patted the old man's hand. "And how are you doing? Pretty good, I guess since they are letting you go home today." Paul did look surprisingly good for someone who had been "run over by a truck," as Charlie had put it (knowing full well it was not actually true). Paul had more or less just been hit by a flying sheep, which had allowed for a much happier outcome. They talked quietly for a while, mostly about the children, Ida Marie Begay and her brother Caleb, who were spending vacation time with Aida Winters up near Cortez.

"I miss those two little magpies." Paul laughed and wondered to himself if they were the reason he had been dreaming of Magpie and Coyote. "Our place is pretty quiet without them."

"I'll bet it is." Sue paused for a moment, not knowing quite how to approach the subject of Harley Ponyboy and his *curse*. Lucy Tallwoman was supposed to have spoken to her father about it but had obviously forgotten, or perhaps didn't want to divulge what she had found out, or maybe just decided everyone's fears were unfounded.

"Shih-chai." She used the Diné word for "father" as a term of respect. "Do you know about Harley Ponyboy and the supposed '*curse*' that is on him?" She looked down at her belly, which seemed to increase in size hourly. "Charlie says it is silliness and to pay it no mind."

The old man nodded but did not look directly at her. "Yes, Charlie Yazzie was away at school for more than most... He may come to think differently in time." Paul paused and looked down at his own hands. "When it comes to Harley Ponyboy, however... he may be right." He smiled. "I have known Harley since he was a boy. He has a strong belief in the old ways—too strong maybe. It may cloud his thinking sometimes. His people were old fashioned; from back in the canyons of *Tsé Bii' Ndzisgaii*-- Monument Valley. They had some strange notions, those people. They hid Harley away and kept him from school most of the time. He sometimes, still thinks like those old people." Paul grimaced, his eyes mere slits, as he thought back. "Thomas knew that man from Ganado who supposedly put the curse on Harley, and he said both of them were drunk at the time and just talking big. Even Thomas does not believe that person was a witch, only a mean-natured little man."

"But what about Anita losing those two babies?"

"Who knows? Sometimes things just happen and no one knows why. Anita was always a sickly girl. Her own mother said she should not try to have children. Her clan did pay for a cleansing ceremony after she lost that first baby, and from a very well-known *singer,* too. It didn't change anything. To me, that means it probably wasn't magic that caused the problem to start with."

Sue thought about this. "That is about what Charlie said too."

"I wouldn't worry yourself about it, daughter." The old man reached over and patted her hand. "That baby will come when he is ready, and he will be fine."

"He? So you think it's a boy too?"

"Yes," Paul chuckled. "I am the one who told Lucy it would be a boy."

"But how…"

"It came to me the day I sprinkled pollen on you and Charlie at your wedding. Something told me your first child would be a boy. That night it came to me again in a dream and I knew then it was true." Paul shifted in his bed and Sue moved to adjust his pillow. "You know, my uncle, whose name I will not mention, as he is dead now, often said he could tell whether a baby would be a boy or girl by how low or high the woman carried it in her belly." The old man showed just a hint of a smile. "My uncle was a famous *singer* in those days and made a good bit of money making such predictions." Paul chuckled. "And he was usually right too—about fifty percent of the time!"

Sue laughed along with him and breathed an audible sigh of relief. "This is a great weight off my shoulders," she said and Paul could see in her eyes it was so and was glad he had not told her everything about the *Witch of Ganado*.

~~~~~~~~

When Sue arrived back home, she found Charlie and Thomas preparing to take George Custer's car to him at Aida Winter's place north of Cortez. They would be gone only for the day, and Lucy Tallwoman had agreed to come stay with Sue until they returned.

Harley Ponyboy was busily putting the final touches on the painted trim in the baby's room when she peeked in on him.

"I'm using a new kind of paint that has no smell to it," he announced. "It's not good for babies to smell that regular kind of paint." He seemed quite proud of this knowledge, and Sue didn't have the heart to tell him latex paint had been around for a while. She was looking at Harley Ponyboy in a different light now and suddenly felt somewhat sorry for him but didn't know exactly why. She wanted to tell him there was no *curse* and Anita losing those babies was due to something else entirely. She couldn't find the words for that though and finally just nodded at him and went out to the kitchen.

Thomas was finishing off the last of Sue's experimental burned toast, dipping it in his coffee, which was heavily laced with canned milk and sugar. "Good toast, Sue! I always liked my toast a little crispy. Makes it just right for dipping."

Sue pursed her lips and smiled. "Glad you like it. I think Charlie was getting a little tired of it." Secretly, she was beginning to think the new toaster was defective. She might have to take it back to K-Mart and get her money back.

"Charlie don't know what's good," Thomas said. "Lucy and I may get us one of these toasters, now that I see how this is."

"You don't have any electricity to run a toaster."

"Sure we do! We have the new generator now. I wouldn't mind firing that thing up in the mornings for a little toast now and then."

Charlie came in just in time to hear the end of the conversation. "Maybe Sue will let you have our toaster. I don't like toast that much, anymore."

Sue turned to Thomas and laughed, "There may be something wrong with that toaster, but you can have it if you want it."

Thomas squinted one eye at the shiny new toaster sitting on the counter. "Seems okay to me." He moved to the counter and appraised the toaster in more detail, "I'll take it!" he decided. Thomas Begay was never one to look a gift horse in the mouth.

When Thomas finally went to see how Harley was getting along with the trim painting, Charlie and Sue were alone. He put his arm around her and whispered, "Hey, I'm sorry about this morning. I didn't mean to be so short with you."

"Aww," Sue said softly and squeezed his arm. "It was mainly me. I've been a little on edge these last few days." Yet, she was not quite ready to tell Charlie about her visit to the old *singer*.

"Well, everything will be better once the baby gets here," Charlie replied, and hoped he was right.

Just then Sue abruptly pulled away, winced in pain, and looked surprised, first at her belly, and then at the spreading puddle at her feet. "Uh-oh," she gasped between clenched teeth. "I think I know what this means!"

Charlie knew what it meant, too, and hurriedly called out to Thomas and Harley who came running—Harley still holding his paint brush which left a trail of light-blue droplets on the new linoleum floor. Both stood with their mouths open at the sight of Sue clutching her stomach in distress. She was clearly concerned, yet in complete control.

Charlie looked momentarily bewildered, but he, too, appeared calm when he said, "You two will have to return George Custer's truck without me. His crew from Albuquerque will be in tomorrow, and he has to be ready to go back up to the dig." He looked from one to the other of them. "It looks like I might be tied up awhile down here." He glanced at Sue in dismay and asked, "How long do you think this might take?" He immediately realized how foolish the question was and threw up his hands. Obviously, Charlie Yazzie, was more excited than he cared to let on.

Harley Ponyboy took a step back when he realized what was happening. He held the paintbrush like a shield, eyes wide with panic.

Thomas Begay, on the other hand, came forward and took Sue's arm. "Do you have a ditch bag, or whatever they call it?" he asked calmly. Sue pointed to the broom closet.

Navajo women are not known for lengthy labor and generally have their babies quickly.

Now, it was Thomas who took charge and ushered Sue and Charlie out the door to the truck. Charlie, clinging desperately to Sue with one hand and to her little blue suitcase with the other, still appeared dazed. Thomas, waving them goodbye, assured them he would take care of everything. "Don't worry about a thing!" he called after them, "I've got this covered!"

Charlie did not find this comforting in the least, and before he pulled up onto the highway, he paused to take a long look back in his rearview mirror—Sue could clearly see doubt etched across his brow.

Harley Ponyboy stood silently on the porch, also watching them go and wringing his hands, as was his wont when overwhelmed by a situation he thought might be construed as his fault.

4

The Expedition

Aida Marie Winters watched intently as George Custer marshaled his troops—a spectacle of near epic proportions. The new recruits scurried around the vans, rearranging supplies and filling small water barrels from Aida's spring-fed pump-house. Harley Ponyboy and Thomas Begay were introduced to all and encouraged to pitch in and help. They soon became swept up in the general melee.

The children found it all highly entertaining and hung on the porch rail watching with obvious excitement. Their previously perceived notion that George Custer was a person of some importance was reinforced by the deference shown him by the entire assemblage. He was clearly held in high regard by these people. Thomas took time to speak with his children and pointed out various interesting things about the group... things they would someday recall in fond remembrance of the day.

Aida took a package of the professor's freshly laundered clothes out to the vehicle and asked Harley to stow them away. It had been fortunate that the bulk of George's clothing had been left forgotten in his truck when he and Harley had started drinking. Aida paused a moment when her attention was attracted by one of the crew, a slender young woman with Indian features and a serious expression—a pretty girl, most would think. There was something vaguely familiar about her, and Aida pondered what it might be. It was almost as though she had known her sometime in the past.

Finally all was in readiness, and Thomas said goodbye to Aida and the children, followed by George Custer, who came and stood before her, hat in hand. "Aida, I want you to know how much I appreciate what you have done for me these last few days." he lowered his eyes, examining the brim of his hat. "Especially in view of what has gone before." He looked her directly in the eye and said, "I would like to make it up to you someday, if that might be possible."

Aida gave George Custer a searching look, then simply turned and walked to the house. The professor did notice a slight slump to her shoulders as she climbed the front steps. And at the top step she paused, looked back over her shoulder, and gave a little half-wave. George Custer thought he perceived the tiniest glint of a tear at the corner of one eye, though the distance was such that he could not be sure.

As the entourage pulled down the lane, children still waving them goodbye, it finally came to Aida why the Indian girl had seemed so familiar. She wondered if George Custer had any idea who she was.

It had not taken much to convince Thomas Begay and Harley Ponyboy to sign on with the second phase of George Custer's project. The pay was good and the job would last through most of the summer. They were sure George Custer would, of necessity, be on his best behavior. The number of university witnesses alone should insure some semblance of professional conduct. The professor had apologized profusely to Harley Ponyboy for his previous behavior and for dragging Harley down with him. George Armstrong Custer was not one to shirk responsibility for his shortcomings.

Upon arriving at the site, the entourage of grad students in their shiny, new four-wheel-drive vans began unpacking the vehicles while the professor and his two Dinè helpers headed up the trail to the campsite.

When they topped out of the wash and could see the camp, Harley Ponyboy, immediately clapped a hand to his mouth and said, "Uh-oh!"

The tent had been slashed to pieces and lay on the ground. Broken camp chairs were strewn about and cooking gear was smashed and scattered to the far edges of the camp. Supplies and food were everywhere, opened and thrown about. When they were closer, it became apparent how thorough the sacking of the camp had been. The papers and grid maps Thomas had so carefully gathered and left in the tent were now a pile of ashes in the fire pit. The two Navajo stood silently surveying the damage and looking to Dr. Custer, who closed his eyes for a moment as though to gather himself. Finally, he gingerly touched his still-bandaged head and said quietly, "Well, it looks like my friends weren't quite through with us after all."

"Could have been a bear." Harley ventured hopefully, knowing for certain that was not the case.

"I doubt a bear would have left those Beanee Weenees," Thomas said, indicating the contents of a number of smashed cans on the ground. "And he might have had a little trouble setting those papers afire, too." Thomas's eyes narrowed as he glared at the mess. "Like the doc says, it was the same people that were here before. They must have been scared off the first time when they heard our truck coming, or they might have finished the job right then and there."

George Custer nodded and said, "The good news is that the crew brought plenty of extra gear and supplies from Albuquerque." George Custer assumed a grim little smile. "This will be a temporary setback, at most." He walked over to the fire pit and sifted through the ashes with one hand. "The worst of it is we lost several days paperwork, and I rather expect the grid markers up at the dig are gone as well." This seemed only momentarily depressing for the professor, and he went on, "Luckily, I've got you boys to fill in. I can put two of the grad students on the paperwork and Harley and I know where a lot of the grid stakes were placed." It was true, Harley had a remarkable memory for minutia, and his sense of place was unerring. This talk left Thomas suspicious that he might be the one to take up the slack in the digging department.

The professor turned to Thomas, "While we are waiting for the others to bring up the gear maybe you and Harley could circle around and see what sort of sign you can turn up before the others get here to muddle things up."

This suited Thomas just fine, and he motioned Harley off to the north as he ambled away in the opposite direction.

"Don't get lost now, Harley," he threw back over his shoulder with a grin.

Harley Ponyboy was an excellent tracker. He'd had plenty of practice when he was off in the canyons as a boy––there wasn't much else to do when you didn't have to go to school. If there was sign to be found, Harley Ponyboy would likely find it.

~~~~~~~

Harley was only about a half mile beyond the camp and well to the northeast of the dig site when he chanced upon a single set of boot prints—large boot prints with squared toes and an aggressive tread pattern. Harley could just make out the Caterpillar brand insignia. Those were some expensive boots. Harley had always wanted such a pair of boots but could never seem to afford them. Boots like these were generally only seen on construction workers, or oil-field hands.

The tracks were heading away from camp. Harley intended to backtrack later, but right now he was more interested in where they were going. He was pretty sure he knew where they had been. It was no more than a mile when two other sets of tracks joined the first. These tracks were different. One set was made by cowboy boots, but with more of a rounded toe, much like the ones Harley himself wore. These were a common style of boot on the reservation and in the surrounding country as a whole. But it was the second set of prints that was most interesting. They appeared to be made by hard-soled moccasins, something you didn't see very much these days outside of the pow-wows and ceremonial gatherings. These days men who didn't wear boots usually wore sneakers. The other thing about the moccasin tracks, they were small, from a youngster, maybe—or a woman. All three sets now led up a draw thick with cedars and oak brush. These people meant to keep out of sight. When the draw eventually topped out, the tracks turned sharply east toward the Ute reservation, and Harley saw the space between the tracks diminish, indicating the people had slowed their pace, perhaps feeling safer at this distance from the destroyed camp. He at last came to a place where the trio had stopped and rested. Two of the people took a seat on a downed log; the third and larger of the three had remained standing and well apart from the others. His prints indicated he had spent his time watching the back trail.

As Harley lingered there in the shade of the cedars the silence cloaked him, enveloped him, until it set up a thin buzzing in his ears. The wind had died, as often happens in the canyons at mid-day—like an ocean tide that comes to slack water and then reverses flow. Harley had nearly transitioned to a state of mental disconnect when the slightest of noises brought him back. He did not quite register what the sound was, only that it didn't belong.

When Thomas finally appeared, he was out of breath and sweating from the steep climb. "I saw you top out and figured you had cut the same two sets of tracks I had seen down below. They were heading this way." He wheezed and bent to catch his breath. "I figured to take a shortcut up the side." He leaned over and, with hands on knees, blew his nose on the ground. "That was a mistake."

Harley smiled, "You are getting old Hastiin. There was ta time when you woulda' *run* up that draw and not been breathing hard like that."

"Yeah, well, then was then—now is now," Thomas wheezed.

Harley looked across the little clearing. "There are three people now. One big fella. This is his track over here. I have to backtrack him to be sure, but I don' know if he ever went down ta the camp. Maybe like he was more of a lookout, or guide, maybe."

Thomas examined the impressions and whistled, "He *is* a big boy, size 12 …14 maybe." Thomas set his size nine boot in the print, and Harley could easily see he was right. Thomas moved on over to the log and peered at the other sets of tracks. "Are these moccasins?"

Harley nodded. "If it hadn't been raining the last few days they would be a lot harder to see." He looked off into the past. "My gran'mother wore moccasins. When her mind finally started ta go she would wander away from ta camp sometimes. If the ground was hard and dry, we had a hell of a time finding her; she only weighed about ninety pounds." Harley pushed his chin at the tracks, "I'm thinking this is a woman too; don' weigh much, neither."

The two started off again and after only half a mile came to the end of the ridge which had slowly angled down and ended at the edge of a patch of sage—an old gas well location by the looks of it. There was still a capped-off standpipe in the center of the circular plot. The "location" was probably one of the first in the Aneth field, now long abandoned and overgrown with sage and cheat grass. What had once been the road leading to it lay washed out and more of a gully than anything. That notwithstanding there was a clear set of vehicle tracks at the far edge. Upon closer inspection it was obvious the tracks were made by a set of oversize mud tires, and it had been at least a day, maybe two, since it was there.

"Someone went to a lot of trouble getting to Dr. Custer's camp without using the main road." Thomas shook his head, "No wonder we never saw any other tire tracks coming in except ours."

Harley stood gazing off into the canyon beyond the well site, studying what was left of the rutted trail coming up out of the bottom. "They din' drive no regular truck in here, neither. It would take one a them Moab rock crawlers to get in here."

"Yep," Thomas agreed, "this was someone who knew this country and how to get around in it." He scratched his head. "I had thought for a while they might have come horseback, but I can see now it would be a long ride in here. You would beat horses to death trying to trailer them anywhere near here."

That evening as the two Navajo came dragging back into George Custer's camp, they were amazed to see how much had been accomplished in so short a time. The place was a beehive of activity; the entire area had been cleaned up and four sleeping tents set along with a larger mess tent. Firewood (including several broken camp chairs) had been gathered and neatly stacked by the fire pit. A blue plastic barrel of drinking water had been collected from the spring and sat near the big tent. It was a good camp. George Custer knew what he was about and how to make things happen, too. There were nine team members, three of them women, but none of them greenhorns. Counting the professor, Thomas, and Harley, that made an even dozen expedition members.

Thomas was parched, and with Harley close behind, went directly to the water barrel. Most Navajo think it silly to carry water for just a day hike, no matter how arduous the terrain. They have been known to go without water for long distances, should they be called upon to do so.

Some fastidious person had installed a dispenser of small paper cups on the side of the water barrel. Harley filled one twice and then just kneeled down and put his mouth under the spigot and had his fill. Thomas was on his fourth little cup when Dr. Custer caught their eye and motioned them over to his new tent, which was set well apart from the others.

"So?" he asked when they had planted themselves on the cedar log beside the tent. "Turn anything up out there?" The professor pulled his campstool in closer, glancing across the compound at the rest of his crew. Several of them were bringing the last loads up from the trucks, as others busied themselves in the mess tent. These were all seasoned people who had been on several previous digs, some of them with Dr. Custer himself.

Thomas related in some detail what they had found. Harley added a few theories along the way that may or may not have been relevant, letting the professor sort them out as he pleased. Harley and George Custer had come to something of a thought-sharing process in their recent drinking days and now understood one another to a remarkable degree.

The odor of cooking wafted its way across the campsite, and Thomas fidgeted, darting glances in the direction of the food. He stood finally and was about to move toward the good smells when he remembered something. Digging in his pocket, he produced a small object on the palm of his hand. He had almost forgotten about it. "I found this following the tracks in the oak brush beyond camp. Must have torn off someone's clothes. I wouldn't have seen it myself if I hadn't caught my own shirt on the same bush and had to look down to undo it."

Harley Ponyboy rose and pushed closer for a look, as did Dr. Custer. "It's a little beadwork," Harley exclaimed, taking it from Thomas's palm. He held it out to Custer while frowning at Thomas for not bringing it to his attention earlier.

"Interesting. It's a boot or moccasin pull, Hopi design... the rain-cloud symbol," and that was all George Custer offered, taking the item and depositing it in his shirt pocket. He had not said a single word during the entire report and now rose without further comment and moved toward the mess tent. The two Navajo fell in behind and exchanged questioning glances.

The people selected for mess duty knew something about camp cooking, and the meal was deemed a resounding success. Thomas and Harley showed their appreciation in the Navajo way—by making sure there were no leftovers.

After a hard day's work, Professor Custer was often inclined to relax with his crew around the campfire, where opinions were expressed, and general small talk bantered about. A portion of this night's talk concerned the empty whiskey bottles the cleanup crew had found. It was generally agreed this was further evidence left by the delinquents that trashed the camp. It was in the volunteer's agreement that no alcohol was allowed in camp, and George Custer and Harley Ponyboy exchanged guarded looks. The professor felt his secret was safe with the two Navajo.

Some of the crew were just getting to know one another, and this night there was lively conversation around the fire. Thomas and Harley were not the only Indians. There was a young Cherokee undergrad named Ted Altman, an even younger Pueblo woman, Tanya Griggs, as well as two Hispanics, one an undergrad from Utah State and the other a South American woman. An older anthropologist, Neva Travis, who taught at a small New Mexico college, was the only white woman. All in all, it was an eclectic mix, and one that would not prove particularly harmonious.

Harley was a bit shy in the company of so many intellectuals and stayed to the outside of the circle and close to Thomas, who while seldom intimidated, seemed hesitant to join in the conversation. The woman anthropologist was particularly determined to draw Thomas out. She reminded him of the white anthropologist who lived with his uncle Johnny up at Navajo Mountain. He liked Marissa—she was almost like family—and she had shown a genuine interest in Lucy Tallwoman and the children. This new professor was a harder copy of Marissa. Thomas avoided her inquiries when he could.

Several of the group had changed their work boots for more comfortable footwear, and all three of the team's women had changed from their work clothes as well. As the evening wore on, Harley Ponyboy occasionally nudged Thomas and pushed his chin toward the other side of the circle. Thomas looked across to see the Pueblo girl and thought for a moment his friend might have designs on her, but that was not likely. Harley was extremely shy around any female and Thomas often wondered how he had ever gotten together with his wife Anita. He could only conclude that they were two of a kind, thrown together by a kind providence. At the third elbow in the ribs, Thomas, irritated at last, turned to Harley and whispered, "What Harley? What?"

Harley looked away for a moment and then again covertly indicated the Hopi girl. This time he raised his eyebrows and then stared pointedly at the girl's feet. Thomas followed his gaze and immediately understood. The girl was wearing knee-high moccasins of a type once very popular among Indian and local white women alike. These particular moccasins had little beaded amulets on the sides, though it was hard to make out the design.

George Custer, perceiving the two Navajos interest in the girl, couldn't help but notice the moccasins as well. Being somewhat closer, he could easily see the small beaded pattern; it was not at all like the one in his shirt pocket. This was not the first time he had seen such moccasins on one of his expeditions.

5

The Bebie

The hospital staff had barely settled Sue Yazzie in her maternity room when her husband advised the head nurse he wanted to be present at the birth. She eyed him up and down and then, with a wry smile asked, "Are you sure you can handle it?" The nurse had never known a Navajo father who wanted to be in the room during a birth. It was not thought proper among older Navajo.

In olden times when no female clan members were available, a woman would just deliver herself of a child and think little of it. Consequently, most Navajo men who found themselves in a modern maternity ward were often quite happy ensconced on a couch in the waiting room, watching television, sometimes the only television they had ever seen on a big, clear screen with good reception.

"I think I can manage." Charlie smiled. "I've delivered a few lambs and foals."

The woman nodded and muttered, "Alright." She pointed through the open door. "I'll let you get suited up after you wash up across the way."

Sue listened from her bed as the nurse told Charlie what he could and couldn't do during the coming birth. It boiled down to just staying quiet and out of everyone's way. Sue was glad he had chosen to stay with her but still was a little apprehensive. He was in an anxious state of mind, and that made her nervous as well. Sue's own birth had been attended only by her aunt, in a dirt-floored Hogan; this, after her mother's five-mile horseback ride to get there. The actual labor took only about forty-five minutes, possibly hastened by the horseback ride.

Sue Yazzie's pains came and went for some hours. Once, when the doctor came in to check on her, Sue spied Lucy Tallwoman and her father in the hallway, being redirected to the waiting area. Paul's recent familiarity with the place had emboldened him to search Sue out. Lucy Tallwoman, a reluctant accomplice, was determined her father not make trouble for her friends.

Paul T'Sosi was still limping from his own recent ordeal, but if this birthing was to end well, he was convinced it would only be with his help. Lucy warned her father they could be thrown out altogether should he not settle down. The old man paid no attention and continued to harangue the orderly sent to retrieve them. Paul clutched a small leather bag beneath his coat and was anxious lest it be discovered. There were things in that bag that could prove harmful in the wrong hands.

By the time Charlie was "suited up" and had figured out the mask and the shoe coverings, things in the delivery room had slowed to a crawl. He was shown to the head of the bed where he took Sue's hand, and as the occasional contractions came and went, she squeezed with all her might. Well into evening, things still were not progressing as expected, and both Sue and Charlie were beginning to wear down. Sue was mildly sedated but told the young doctor she did not want a spinal block or even an epidural, if it could be avoided. She and Charlie had discussed this a number of times during the pregnancy, and it was Sue's thinking that she could do without that sort of thing. She said her mother had only a piece of cedar wood wrapped in soft leather to bite down on when she was born. This would be the first baby in Sue's family to be born in a hospital. Charlie, too, had been born at home. They agreed this could be done without heavy sedation and felt the natural way might still be the best way. After all, it had worked for their people since their very beginning.

The attending physician was not their regular doctor (already in the midst of another delivery some miles away). The on-call doctor seemed quite young yet appeared to be in control of the situation. Charlie couldn't see past the tented sheet but did hear him ask for various instruments with long names, none of which sounded indicative of a normal birth.

The baby's head was nearly out before Charlie allowed himself to think the worst might be over—for him anyway. He was now sweating nearly as much as Sue and mopped both their brows with the same gauze pad. He occasionally leaned over, offered encouragement, and helped Sue sip water through a straw.

The doctor mumbled something under his breath, causing the two nurses to move in closer. Charlie thought he heard one say something about the *cord*.

From down the hall there was the faint sound of singing—Navajo singing. Old Paul T'Sosi was conducting a prayer vigil in the waiting room, much to the consternation of several white visitors, one of whom eventually reported the matter. The beleaguered orderly was again sent to see what could be done about the old man. He was soon back, shaking his head, and saying he had done what he could and could do no more. He was Navajo himself, and when the old man offered to include him in the incantations (and not in a good way), the orderly felt it best not to interfere further with the old man's magic.

At the foot of the bed the doctor looked up and, for just an instant, Charlie thought he saw something in his eyes—something that caused him to catch his breath.

~~~~~~~

West of Aneth at George Custer's camp, Harley Ponyboy sat bolt upright in a cold sweat. He took a moment to collect his thoughts and recall the dream. It had been filled with bad images, which even now caused his skin to crawl and his heart to race. He rose and quietly made his way by moonlight far into the outlying cedars, to a place he might find a bit of sage and have a little fire without being seen. Harley Ponyboy was quite a religious person, in his own way. Navajo religion is a rather loose affair at best and may often vary from place to place, and even clan to clan. There is no written protocol in regard to appeasing the gods. The various deities and their involvement in the affairs of man are subject to individual interpretation, for the most part. While there are set guidelines for the ceremonies that deal with particular evils, a private appeal to the gods is a very personal matter, and each person generally must find his own way in the thing.

Harley Ponyboy knew many of the old prayer songs and even the accepted way in which to approach the deities. His family went back, almost directly, to the first people and had kept all the old traditions alive when others had let them fall by the wayside. If he had, in any way, caused harm to the Yazzie's baby, he meant to fix it this night.

Harley Ponyboy and Thomas Begay had chosen to sleep out beyond the perimeter of the camp, since the weather was good, and neither felt comfortable in the space allotted them at the back of the mess tent. Professor Custer had earlier insisted they bunk in his tent, but both declined, Thomas saying they had spent the better part of their lives sleeping in a brush "summer hogan" in good weather and that is where they slept best.

Thomas Begay, a light sleeper when sober, lay awake in his blankets but did not follow after Harley Ponyboy when he left the camp. He knew Harley had been worried about Sue and the baby. This was something Harley Ponyboy would have to do alone. Thomas recalled his Uncle John Nez once saying, "A man must sometimes meet with his devils and talk them down to size." Thomas had no idea what he meant by the saying. Uncle Johnny had fought in Viet Nam and had picked up several unusual ideas over there. *Uncle Johnny would have made a good code-talker; if there had been code-talkers in that war.*

When Thomas again woke, it was to the muffled clang of the breakfast triangle. He saw that his friend Harley, was back in his blankets and smelled of sage and wood smoke. His face was streaked with charcoal. The little man wore a faint smile of contentment and snored noisily. Harley Ponyboy had been praying in the only way he knew how; the old way.

~~~~~~

In the end, the umbilical cord was found to be the culprit impeding the birth of Sue and Charlie Yazzie's baby. It had wrapped around his neck and eventually required several manipulations by the uncertain young doctor. When it finally came, it was indeed a boy and as worn out as its parents. Charlie and Sue were both relieved and revitalized by the sight and cries of their new son— though they had only a glimpse before he was swept away to the ICU.

Sue would later say, "I knew that baby was doing some flips in there. Maybe I was drinking too much coffee and that's how he got that cord wrapped around his neck."

The doctor smiled, looking somewhat older now, and said, "The baby's breathing seems a little shallow, and he will require a short time in an incubator until stabilized." He noted the new parents' concern. "Not long," he said, stripping off his mask and gloves and rubbing his jaw with a hand that still shook slightly. Charlie was ushered out of the delivery room after a quick kiss for Sue, who offered up a wan smile in spite of the ordeal.

The nurse told Charlie she was proud of the way he had held up. After Sue was cleaned up and taken to her new room, she would advise them as to how the new baby should be held and cared for. Charlie somehow resented this and though he had never actually held a baby and didn't know if Sue had either, he thought it should be a natural enough inclination. He already had seen the doctor hold the child up by the legs and give it a little swat to jumpstart it's breathing. How far off could he and Sue be from holding it properly?

When Sue was taken out of the room, the doctor motioned Charlie into the hall and said confidentially, "That baby was in trouble for a while." He bit his lower lip and went on almost hesitantly, "I was afraid he wasn't getting enough oxygen." He chuckled nervously. "I've never really had a delivery like this. The baby seemed to be in some sort of struggle, first strong and then weak, as though something was pulling him first one way and then another." He turned to go, then, over his shoulder, said, "Someone was watching over that baby. That's for sure."

Charlie slumped against the wall for a moment and then went to the end of the long corridor, where he found Lucy Tallwoman and her father alone in the waiting room.

Lucy smiled guiltily as he came in and said with a sweep of her hand, "I think we might have run a few people off."

Her father, who appeared to be dozing, sat up at this. "Well, they missed a good chance to learn something then." He smiled, nodding his head in Charlie's direction, "How's that new baby?"

Charlie had to smile himself. "He's fine, or will be soon. They said we could all go in and see them as soon as he's had a whiff or two of oxygen."

"How's Sue doing?" Lucy stood and touched Charlie's shoulder. "She was a long time in labor. My dad almost ran out of prayers, I think."

Charlie gazed thoughtfully at the old man for a moment, "Well, I'm glad he didn't. We needed all the help we could get in there."

The old man grinned. "That is a fine-looking doctor suit you have there, I wouldn't mind having one of those for when I make house calls."

Later, when the orderly peeked in, he looked only at Charlie and avoided the glare of the old man. "The nurse says you people can come back up to your wife's room now, if you want. The baby should be along shortly. They said he perked right up in that incubator."

Charlie heaved a sigh of relief and thanked the young man.

Old Paul T'Sosi scowled at the orderly until the young Navajo grew nervous and left the room. When his daughter frowned at him, he gestured at the open doorway. "That boy is in need of some manners when it comes to his elders."

As they trooped into Sue's new room she was already holding her son and smiling and cooing at the small red face. All the statistics were revealed, and Charlie was quite proud of the fact that at eight pounds the baby was the largest born in several days—this according to the head nurse, who seemed a bit proud of him herself. The nurse gently took the baby from Sue and showed Charlie exactly how to hold the infant before passing it over. He gingerly took the child and showed it all around. The baby looked blearily up at Charlie, and a little smile appeared on its tiny lips.

Lucy Tallwoman's old father watched closely and whispered, "There is an old Dinè saying: 'The first person to make a new baby smile, will always be that baby's hero.'"

Lucy tilted her head, teared up, and murmured, "Awww."

Paul looked more closely at the baby. "Or it could just be a gas bubble."

It was only twelve days after the baby was born that Sue decided Charlie was getting on her nerves and that it might be best for all concerned should he take a little trip somewhere, maybe up to see George Custer. He had already used up his vacation time and had taken extra time off to stay home with Sue and the new arrival. He hovered around Sue constantly to see if she needed anything and was forever picking up his son to check his diaper and listen to his breathing. Sue was afraid Charlie's constant messing with him was keeping the baby from his sleep.

Lucy Tallwoman came as often as she could, but her father was still somewhat weak from his recent sheep-wreck, and she was loath to leave him alone for very long.

Charlie's great aunt, Annie Eagletree, had hoped to come immediately after the birth to help out until Sue felt okay with things. But her husband Clyde had come down with a cold, and she decided she didn't need to bring any sickness around the baby. By the time they finally did show up, Charlie was suffering from a severe case of "cabin fever" and was anxious to see how things were progressing up at George Custer's dig near Aneth. He especially wondered how Thomas and Harley were getting on and if there had been any more trouble.

Aunt Annie and Clyde, when they arrived, brought their own housing with them—an eight-by-ten sheepherder tent with a little sheet-metal wood stove. That stove came in handy, Annie said, whenever they could find wood for it. They pitched the tent in the back yard, and Clyde immediately went to work on the garden, which was beginning to show signs of neglect. Clyde, who had once fancied himself a farmer, (though not a very good one, some thought), decided he could show his educated nephew a trick or two about gardening. Annie Eagletree, watching from the kitchen window, shook her head and had her doubts.

Sue didn't feel she needed help at this point but knew Charlie needed a break, and would be easier in his mind if his aunt and uncle were there to look after them. Aunt Annie might be a "cop-show" junkie, but she knew a lot about babies, too, and was still quite spry for one of her years. She was the sort of take-charge, old-school *Dinè* woman that reminded Sue of her own mother.

Only a few days after the baby was brought home, Thomas Begay had called from the market in Blanding, where he had been sent to gather more food and supplies for George Custer's camp.

After hearing all about the new baby, he filled Charlie in on the goings on at the dig, including the latest ransacking of the camp and what little they had discovered about the intruders. The new crew did not know about the previous assault on the professor and thought the ravaged camp the work of vandals, probably young delinquents from one of the area towns.

Charlie left for Aneth the morning following his relatives' arrival, but not before Annie cornered him on the subject of forensics and what his take might be in regard to ballistic tests on shotguns. Charlie allowed, rightly enough, that he had never heard of any ballistic test for shotguns due to the fact that they shot... well, shot, pellets not bullets, and there was really no way to associate spent shot with one particular shotgun barrel. Charlie had never owned a shotgun himself and had little interest in them.

"HA!" Aunt Annie snorted. "My TV show last week said there is a way. It all has to do with patterning the shot at different distances." She folded her arms across her chest, and Charlie knew she was spoiling for a fight. Ordinarily, he would have obliged her, as he knew how much she enjoyed it, but he didn't have time for it this day. He just nodded agreement to the possibility and went on gathering his gear for the trip up-country. Annie had expected more of an argument out of him. She and he had been arguing with each other since he was six years old, and she was now disappointed that he would not give a better account of himself.

~~~~~~~

The next morning Charlie was nearly to the Aneth cutoff when he saw black clouds, *Thunderbirds*, building to the northwest. *If there were much rain in those clouds the rutted track into camp might soon be impassable. And once there, it might be awhile before anyone would be able to get out.* He kicked the truck up to sixty-five and held it there until he hit the gravel turnoff.

Charlie had some serious reservations concerning the safety of the Professor and his crew. *If the attempt on George Custer's life was any indicator, things could turn ugly.* With this latest incident reported by Thomas, he was more concerned than ever. He had been giving this a lot of thought lately, especially after reading Dr. Custer's latest paper, which had apparently been mailed from his office before he left Albuquerque.

When he wasn't changing diapers or fixing supplemental bottles, Charlie studied the professor's latest paper and was convinced it would prove to be a very controversial take on the Anasazi Migration. *There were definitely some pretty creative suppositions in the work— the sort of things that might raise the ire of certain people. Someone obviously had it in for the professor already, and clearly it had something to do with the excavation of the Anasazi site.*

6

The Bigfoot

As George Custer directed the re-gridding of the site, Harley Ponyboy paid close attention, several times offering suggestions based on the memory of their previous work, suggestions that proved deadly accurate and saved a great deal of time. The professor liked this *Dinè* and regretted his part in the recent lapse in the man's sobriety. Harley himself, however, appeared to have come to terms with his recent fall from grace and appeared ready to move beyond it. George Custer himself, on the other hand, desperately wanted a drink and was pretty sure he knew where to get one.

Thomas Begay grubbed sagebrush from the low mound of what had once been a middens or refuse heap for the ancient village. He tried not to be jealous of Harley's suddenly elevated position. He had learned long ago that jealous thoughts led to a loss of hozo. It seemed strange that this change in fortune should come about mainly through drinking. In any case, Thomas felt content with his work and remained thankful for any job in these tough times on the reservation.

The Hopi girl and the woman from South America were helping with resetting the grid markers and laying string from one stake to another. The professor watched the Indian girl with a quizzical, somewhat critical eye, possibly indicating the girl might not have been his personal choice for this project.

When lunchtime came, Thomas and Harley carried their sandwiches and bottles of water over to the shaded log by the professor's tent; they thought it too warm in the mess tent. Mess duty was a revolving responsibility, and today's crew was not as experienced as the one the night before. Those cheeseburgers and baked beans had been delicious, in Harley's view, and he could hardly wait until it was he and Thomas's turn to cook. He had a few tricks up his sleeve, he told Thomas, if he could just get his hands on the right stuff.

As they munched their peanut butter and jelly sandwiches, Thomas thought again of the girl with the moccasins but could not recall her name and finally asked Harley, "Did you happen to catch that Hopi girl's name?"

"Yes," Harley said, thinking only a moment, "it is Tanya... Tanya Griggs but she is called "Little Bird" by the Hopi." Harley's memory was remarkable and it never failed to surprise Thomas. Back when the two had been drinking and Thomas could sometimes barely remember his own name, Harley Ponyboy—while just as drunk—would help arresting officers correctly fill in all Thomas's details on the detention form.

Harley grinned. "From what the professor says he didn't even know she was coming 'til she got here."

"That's right," George Custer, declared, lifting the tent flap. "I didn't know she was coming." Both Navajo jumped slightly at this, neither knowing the professor was in the tent and listening. The professor threw back the flap and came to take a seat in his camp chair. "She was a last-minute addition to the roster by the department head. There was still a position open when I left, and the old bastard felt this girl was qualified. He seemed to think we might be shorthanded without her. There was no way to get in touch with me at the time, of course—for obvious reasons." He smiled and went on, "Something has been bothering me about that girl from the moment I laid eyes on her. I didn't recognize her name—and still don't for that matter. He eyed the camp, then continued. "I was just having a look at her resume when I heard you boys talking." Here he lowered his voice and glanced over his shoulder. "Turns out I may know something about her after all." There was a good bit more the professor might have said, but he caught himself and didn't. He regarded the pair silently for a moment, turned abruptly, and entered his tent without comment, pulling down the flap behind him. Thomas looked at Harley, smiled and shrugged—*white people.*

~~~~~~~~

Charlie arrived at the wash below the camp just as a little wall of foaming water hissed and spit its way out of a side canyon to spread out across the floor of the wash. He shifted into four-wheel drive and tried to stay out of the ruts. It was not raining here yet, but Charlie knew it was raining upstream somewhere. This wash could easily become dangerous if it continued.

Two of Custer's work crew had just managed to pull their vehicles up to slightly higher ground as Charlie eased up out of the wash. The pair stood on the upper bank and stared suspiciously at him until they spotted the tribal emblem on his truck. They waved him on up the slight incline and guided him into the only space left on the little bench. Charlie thought, *Good thing someone had the good sense to see this coming. This was the sort of late spring storm that could bring a real gully washer.* He was glad he had taken his old yellow rain slicker off his saddle and hoped the others in camp were equipped for the coming weather as well.

When he and the two volunteers finally straggled into camp, the rain had begun in earnest. The rest of the crew was ditching around tents to divert the runoff and retrieving clothes and blankets that had earlier been hung out to air.

Charlie spotted Thomas and Harley across the camp, helping unroll thin sheets of Visqueen plastic to throw over the ridgepoles and down the sides of the tents. The professor maintained it was the only way to keep them snug and dry in periods of wet weather. Once again George Custer's foresight and experience in this rugged and isolated country had shown him to be the right man for the job.

Thomas saw Charlie first and shouted across for him to drop his duffle in the mess tent and come help. By the time the tents were secured, everyone was soaking wet and gathered around the big cook tent's wood stove, which was woofing and rattling smoke up the stovepipe. The smell of blazing cedar on the damp breeze was comforting to those who had spent a portion of their lives in such a camp.

George Custer was still in his tent finishing some paperwork, but Thomas and Harley immediately came to clap Charlie on the back and congratulate him on the new *ahwayh.*

Just the week before Thomas, had gone to Blanding for supplies and took the opportunity to call Charlie "collect" from the payphone outside the market. He wanted to know all about the baby and when assured all was well, said that would be a load off poor Harley's mind. According to Thomas, he had thought of little else the past week.

When the cooks announced the meal was nearly ready, Charlie volunteered to go for the professor—he wanted to surprise him. He had told Thomas on the phone that he would be there as soon as possible, if only for a few days, but Dr. Custer had no idea he was coming. As Charlie, in his yellow slicker, noisily slogged his way through the storm, he saw a movement from the corner of his eye and imagined he saw a shadowy figure at the back of the professor's tent. The apparition became aware of Charlie at the same instant and melted silently into the woods. Charlie stopped, caught his breath, and then ran to throw open the tent-flap expecting to find—he knew not what.

George Armstrong Custer looked up from his makeshift desk in astonishment and pushed his glasses up on his nose. "Charlie!" he shouted and grinned hugely at his former student.

Charlie pointed a finger at him. "Stay there, George, I'll be right back," he said, and then rushed out of the tent and around the side. The pelting rain had already melted whatever sign there may have been. He could barely make out the large, shallow depressions behind the tent and was unable to make any sense of them. He was about to turn away when a long, thin wail came on the wind. And then nothing.

George Custer was standing beside him now, in his shirtsleeves, already soaking wet. "What!" he cried. "What was that?"

"I don't know." Charlie's voice was only a whisper as he peered into the darkness, then shook his head. "I've never heard anything like it." He pointed into the dark. "I saw someone—or something, there behind your tent. Whatever it was ran when it saw me. And then there was that scream, or howl. Something."

When Charlie and Dr. Custer made their way to the mess tent, the professor paused for a moment at the entrance and touched Charlie on the arm. "I would appreciate it if you didn't say anything to the others about this. No reason to get everyone stirred up." He looked up the incline to the ruins. "You can tell Harley and Thomas if you want. They already know a lot of what's going on, but not the others. I'll fill you in tomorrow."

The cook tent was warm and bright with lantern light, and everyone was already seated at the long folding table. The two cooks were dishing up steaming bowls of rich, red chili con carne and passing out metal trays stacked with wedges of warm, sweet-smelling cornbread. The number-one mess crew was on duty and had kept the sheet-metal oven at a perfect temperature, a feat few others had been capable of.

Harley Ponyboy grinned because this was one of his favorite meals. He had become a huge fan of this particular set of cooks. The woman anthropologist from New Mexico was in charge, and she smiled at the praise from the tired, wet crew. She threw an inquiring glance at Thomas, but he was already stuffing his face and failed to notice. The woman seemed fascinated by Thomas and Harley. She was from far to the south and was unfamiliar with the Navajo. Most of her work had been with the southern Apache bands east of the Gila. She was curious how these Athabaskan cousins differed from one another.

Charlie was seated between Harley Ponyboy and Thomas Begay, directly across from the Hopi girl, Tanya Griggs. They had been introduced earlier but only in passing. Charlie looked across at her now and asked, "How is your mother?"

Professor Custer, who was sitting next to the girl, put down his butter knife and stared first at the girl, then at Charlie. "Do you two know each other?"

The girl shot Charlie a quizzical glance but remained silent.

Charlie smiled and said, "I was with the Navajo tribal delegation that visited Walpi to discuss joint tribal grazing issues. That's been several years ago. I recall you and your mother wore traditional dress and looked very much alike." Charlie took a sip of water and continued, "Your father, the tribal archivist, I believe, spoke on traditional rights your people felt were key to their position in the negotiations."

The girl frowned then brightened. "Yes, I was there taking notes and helping my mother. She was translating for some of the elders." Tanya was not at first reticent but grew slightly more guarded as she went on. "There was quite a crowd of you Navajo there that day. I don't recall you specifically, but I do remember the meeting." She looked sideways at Professor Custer and her eyes narrowed. "I believe you, also, knew my mother... once worked together on several projects." She noted the professor's raised eyebrows, "Her name is Myra Griggs now, but you may remember her as Myra Santos. She was a UNM grad student and later an anthropologist with the state."

Doctor Custer nervously cleared his throat and feigned surprise, "Oh, of course, I remember Myra. And now I know why you seemed so familiar. You do look like your mother, now that I recall." George Custer did remember Myra Santos, and more.

There had been one person who was happy at the turn of events on Aida Winter's ranch that summer he was called away to Guatemala: Hopi anthropologist Myra Santos. She had mistakenly thought, at the time, that his leaving might be the answer to her dilemma.

Myra Santos had petitioned his department head to be included in his expedition on the grounds her work was closely aligned with his. They had gotten along well in the beginning. Later, however, they had come to loggerheads when he made clear the direction his new research was taking. Research regarding some rather disturbing evidence found in certain kiva excavations and linked directly to the final migration period. Myra Santos felt the work had the potential to reflect badly on her people and begged him not to publish it. *It was irrelevant how the research might reflect on anyone. It was a matter of science.* George was adamant in that regard.

At home, in Walpi village on First Mesa, Myra Santos was called Chosovi, which means "Bluebird" in the Hopi tongue. In later years she was to become the wife of white anthropologist, Dr. Steven Griggs, who served as the Hopi cultural archivist. While Hopi women hold a high place in the matrilineal society, as a whole, there still are many cultural and ceremonial matters that are forbidden to them. It was an odd juxtaposition that, while Myra Santos had herself been refused the position of archivist on the grounds that she was a woman, her husband was hired but censored and denied certain information, due to being white.

There is reason to believe large areas of Hopi cultural information remain the secret domain of the various cloistered men's societies. Even more discouraging for anthropologists and archaeologists alike is that a number of today's scholars feel much of the information passed down has been so distorted by time and "word of mouth" transmission, that it is nearly useless in the context of a deeper understanding of their Anasazi forbears. The intrusion of the loose coalition of Athabaskans, who would later evolve into the Navajo/Apache around 1300, had no doubt left its genetic influence on later Pueblo people—just as the Pueblo had on the Navajo and Apache. The Spanish *entrada* (entrance), which may have occurred as early as the mid-1500's, in that part of the country, was particularly disruptive of the entire Pueblo culture and further diluted the gene pool, leaving some to believe less than a ghost of similarity might remain between present-day Hopi beliefs and their ancient Anasazi ancestors. Hopi and other Pueblo people hotly deny this. Scholars point out that the Zuni and Hopi both claim the same Anasazi ancestry, but indeed are quite different people—Hopi springing from the Shosonian language rootstock as is the Uto-Aztecan language group. The Zuni language is isolate, but with elements of the Penutian language groups. Even today they are culturally quite different, with the Hopi having a much more complex culture centered specifically on a religion that affects every facet of their lives.

It was little wonder that Professor Custer had not immediately recognized Myra Santos's daughter. It had been some years since he had last seen Myra, and her new last name did not ring a bell either. He remembered her being rather dark, with the short stature of her people, while this girl, Tanya, was lighter and slightly taller than most Hopi and with finer features. She had obviously thrown to her father's side of the family and might well have been taken for a Hispanic, or even an Anglo, in the context of other surroundings. Still, she did resemble her mother in many subtle ways, and the Professor felt remiss in not picking up on them. Her eyes were much like her mother's, and she walked in the same graceful manner. Her resumé revealed she was an undergrad student with a double major in both anthropology and archaeology. She came to them from Arizona State with impeccable references and very good grades. Given her parents accomplishments there would have been little reason for the department head to deny her a place on the project.

~~~~~~~

The next morning dawned cloudy with the promise of more rain. A sharp north wind tore the clouds to rags and sent them flying across the canyons like witches. Charlie Yazzie, along with Harley Ponyboy and Thomas Begay, tried once more to pick up the trail of the previous evening's intruder but found it impossible to determine more than a general direction of travel, and even that turned out to be a ruse. While the rain-washed tracks circled away to the south, it was soon clear they later swung back to the northeast, just as the original assailant's tracks had. Harley Ponyboy was most interested in the size of the tracks and the wild wailing noises Charlie had described. Harley was a confirmed fan of the "Sasquatch" genre of TV movies. "Big foots are real," he declared and would not be convinced otherwise. Charlie and Thomas Begay smiled at Harley for this, though Thomas was not as confident as Charlie. Thomas still believed in Shape-Shifters or Yeenaaldiooshii, just as Harley did. *If such as them were out-and-about, why not Big Foots?*

Thomas brought up the original interloper they had tracked, the one making the big tracks. "What about him,

Harley? He could have made those tracks. Tracks always look bigger in the mud. You know that."

"Yeah," Harley hedged, "but we don't know he wasn't a Bigfoot either."

Thomas and Charlie just looked at one another and shook their heads.

~~~~~~

The camp was taking a "lay" day due to the weather, and there was very little activity at the excavation site. About half the crew had forgotten to bring rain gear, and there was a run on the supply of black plastic garbage bags from the mess tent. With holes cut for the head and arms, they made fairly efficient rain protection. Harley and Thomas both had one and thought it silly that some people spent money on expensive rain suits. Rain gear was not generally considered a requirement for reservation living.

After lunch, the three Navajo met with Professor Custer to go over a set of topographic maps of the area. Charlie was particularly interested in the old gas-well location the original intruders were tracked to. He whistled when he saw the distance from the well head to the nearest maintained road and said, "It's hard to believe these people would make such a rough trip in here on a regular basis. It's pretty much a given that they have had this camp under surveillance for a while." Charlie tapped a finger on one particular area of the map. "I'm thinking they have their own camp somewhere down the east side of the mesa."

Thomas thought he might be right. "When this weather lifts, I think a couple of us should take another little jaunt over there and scope out that lower canyon. They might be using that 'rock crawler' just to get up the mesa and then come in here from a base camp on foot."

Charlie studied the map a bit more and concluded, "It's still a hell of a long way over here, even from that wellhead." He shook his head. "These people are deadly serious."

George Custer leaned over to study the area Charlie was talking about. "There *is* also the chance they could have a small spike camp a lot closer than we think. There is some very rough country just to the east of us."

As the professor leaned over and traced out several vague trails through the far canyon, Charlie got the distinct impression he could smell alcohol. Charlie hated to think the professor would take such a risk again, and so soon after his near disaster.

Charlie had accepted Dr. Custer's offer to bunk in his tent, partially to keep an eye out for trouble and partially because the available space in the mess tent had shrunk. The wet weather had driven Thomas and Harley inside the last few nights, and the other tents were full as well.

George Custer looked at his packing-box desk with its pile of papers and sighed. "There should be a fresh pot of coffee over in the cook tent. Why don't you boys go have some and warm up?"

Charlie grabbed his slicker off his cot and asked, "You coming George?"

"No, I have some paperwork I need to clear up. I'll be along for supper."

When the three were once again back out in the rain and about halfway to the mess tent, Charlie turned to Thomas and asked, "You didn't buy the prof. any booze when you were in town, did you?"

"So you smelled it too!" Thomas confirmed Charlie's suspicion but was a little put out that his friend would suspect him—but then, he *did* have a track record.

Charlie caught the tone of his reply but went on, "Who else went to town for supplies last week?" Charlie saw this new wrinkle as an added complication to an already serious situation.

Thomas didn't have to think about this and said, "Only Harley and that anthropologist woman from Silver City—Neva Travis. They were the only ones to come along with me."

Harley piped up, "She said the womens needed supplies, you know, 'lady stuff' an' I didn' want to know no more." He screwed up his face at Charlie. "I din' buy no booze neither. I didn' even have no money."

"Ya know," Thomas mused, "I been suspecting several of these people of maybe having a little nip now and then. They been way too happy, in my opinion. Any of them could have brought it in with 'em."

Harley, who seldom spoke ill of anyone, said, "All's I know, that Neva Travis woman makes damn fine chili." And that was his final word on the matter.

The woman in question was at the cook stove when they went into the mess tent and, after pouring themselves steaming cups of coffee the three Navajo took seats at the far end of the table by the sugar bowl and canned milk. As they adjusted their coffee (heavy on the sugar), they cast furtive glances at the anthropologist and each evaluated her, individually, and differently.

Finally, Charlie wondered out loud if the professor might still have a bottle hidden out from when they hauled him away the first time.

Harley pondered this, "Maybe, he is a very smart man an' is good at plann'n' ahead." And then he sheepishly admitted, "One reason I came to town was I thought the booze was about gone anyway."

Thomas sighed and admitted, "I guess a hideout bottle is a possibility. I know I used to keep one myself."

Harley, a staunch defender of Professor Custer when he had anything to work with, volleyed back, "Well, ya know, the doc is hell on patting on that stuff, Bay Rum, after he shaves, or when he don' have time to clean up good." He slapped the table. "Maybe that's what you two smelled."

Thomas squinted one eye at the canvas ceiling and was silent. Charlie nodded and smiled. "Maybe, Harley... maybe."

As the crew filed in for supper, Charlie covertly appraised each in turn and occasionally asked his companions something regarding one or the other of them. The two knew very little, actually, and had, so far, worked with only a few of those in question.

Harley was counting them off as they came in and whispered "Nine" when the last one took his seat. "Hmmm, Thomas and me makes eleven, and ta professor makes an even dozen." Then his eyes widened, and he turned to look at Charlie Yazzie with a hint of suspicion. "You make thirteen, Charlie..." and waited for the implication to sink in. Even Navajos view the number 13 as being unlucky, or worse.

Charlie rolled his eyes, but Thomas looked suspiciously at him now, as well, and said seriously, "That could be a sign, Charlie," and paused to grin, "A sign that Harley is a nut," and broke into a laugh. "But, we already knew that!" Several of the nearest white people turned their heads and glanced their way. There was a lot of curiosity about these Indian friends of the professor.

Harley Ponyboy scowled at his friend and shook a finger. "Someday you gonna find you are not so smart as you think!"

Professor Custer came in about then and took his place at the head of the table. "Folks there are just a few things I think we should address this evening." He stopped to gaze around the table. "Some lion tracks have been spotted outside camp, and you may have heard it squalling. It appears he's intent on hanging around, and until we decide otherwise, I believe it would be prudent to only leave camp in pairs. I know we often see lion sign out here, but this may be an old male that has lost his ability to bring down a deer. He may be looking for easier prey—that could be you. So just keep an eye out and try not to be out there alone." He rubbed his healing eyebrow with the back of his hand. "And if you notice anything unusual, please let me know."

There was a general murmur among the crew but no real concern—most all of them had seen lion tracks over the years.

Thomas grinned at Charlie and whispered, "Well, that should cover the noises in the night and any strange sign out there."

Harley smiled grimly and whispered back, "I tol' you he was smart."

The professor had almost sat back down when he thought of something else and stood again. "After dinner this evening I will give a short talk on the main thrust of our work here and what it is we are looking for. I know you all read your 'introduction' to the expedition when you signed on." He canted his head and grinned. "At least I hope you have." This brought smiles and light laughter. "But I have some further and more detailed information I would like you to bear in mind as excavation continues." He waved a hand at the assemblage signifying he was indeed through speaking this time and sat down.

After the meal everyone helped clean up and then returned to their places at the table. Cups of fresh coffee were passed around, and there was a platter of Oreo cookies at each end of the table. Harley gathered a small pile of them on a napkin and placed them between him and Thomas, then smiled and gave George Custer his full attention.

"People," Dr. Custer announced as the conversation fell off, "as you know, our expedition goal is to verify this site as one of a string of transitory waypoints along the final migration routes." He paused for emphasis. "When certain bands of Anasazi found it impossible to maintain their agrarian lifestyle in this area a general exodus ensued, eventually leaving the entire Four Corners virtually abandoned. This may have taken no more than fifty or sixty years, which is remarkable when one considers the scope of the exodus." The professor took a sip of coffee and looked pointedly about the table, his gaze seeming to linger on the young Hopi woman, Tanya Griggs, as he said, "It was not a gradual withdrawal taking many generations, but rather a concerted, relatively rapid transition, exacerbated by violence and fear."

There were some murmurings among the gathering, as many were aware of Dr. Custer's reputation for unorthodox views on the subject.

Charlie leaned over to Thomas and said, "Here it comes."

Then to everyone's surprise the Professor proceeded through a rather bland talk, enumerating the various other escape routes (mainly along the great river courses—the Rio Grand, Colorado, and their tributaries). It was as though it occurred to him that he already might have divulged certain information prematurely. Many knew the Professor's personal agenda concerned a paper—due out in only a few months—on this very subject. The professor continued, mostly regarding technical procedures and methodology that were to be applied to the excavation, notably in connection with the main kiva. "I want to caution those working in the kiva to proceed with extra care, as I expect some rather delicate material to be unearthed." This last revelation caused another slight buzz, for they wondered what the professor might already know.

Charlie Yazzie turned to Harley Ponyboy and whispered. "Harley, are you on the kiva crew?"

"No," Harley murmured, "Professor Custer said me and Thomas don't have the experience yet for that kind of digging."

Thomas Begay added, "Sounds like the professor already has a pretty good idea of what he's going to find up there."

Charlie, watching the professor, thought he looked tired and said quietly, "Keep in mind, this is the fourth Anasazi site the Professor has tracked on the migration route, starting with the one on Aida Winters Ranch. I think he has a pretty good idea what he may find, and will be pretty disappointed if he doesn't.

The next morning dawned bright and clear, with a fresh breeze out of the west. Harley Ponyboy, who was sent to check on the vehicles, reported back that runoff water had barely reached the hubcaps on the trucks, and he thought the wash would be passable again within twenty-four hours at the most if there was no more rain. This was better news than Charlie Yazzie had hoped for, but when Harley went on to say he had also found tracks on the ridge above the vehicles, he was not so pleased.

"It was *not* a 'Bigfoot,' I guess," Harley grinned, "Unless 'Bigfoots' wear new Caterpillar boots."

After talking this over, Charlie and Thomas figured it might be a good time to further investigate the possibility of an unfriendly camp—one within striking distance.

~~~~~~~

Aida Marie Winters had fallen under a general malaise of spirit after George Custer's entourage pulled out, and she didn't quite know why. Now, as she sat on her veranda watching the two children at play down at the corrals, she was further reminded of how very lonely it would be when they were gone. The two children were hanging on the top rail of the corral, discussing Aida's current crop of horseflesh. Both children had been around horses all their young lives, and early on, learned from their Ute cousins how to behave around stock. *Ida Marie Begay, like her father, Thomas, was already a good judge of a horse and could ride like a, well, like a wild Indian. Caleb Begay rode nearly as well but was not yet as fearless as his older sister.*

The sibling's conversation, mostly in English, drifted up to Aida on the morning breeze. It sounded like the twittering of little birds. As she listened, she gazed down at the board flooring of the veranda. She thought she could almost see the stains where their mother, Sally Klee, had been shot down from the far ridge above the house. It had taken a lot of scrubbing to get those stains out of the pine boards, but there was no way to erase them from her mind. The Buck clan had paid dearly for that. The deaths of George Jim and Hiram Buck, each at the hands of the other, had caused the remainder of the clan to gradually fall apart. Slowly, almost without realizing it was happening, they began to disperse. They had come to believe the Buck property was cursed and, one by one, the families sold their small plots to Aida and moved on, a few to join their relatives on the Uinta reserve and others to nearby towns. The Bucks were not Southern Ute, as many thought, but were of the northern bands and had only settled in that country due to the good fortune of an early patriarch who had gained a foothold in the old Ute land allotments.

Aida rose, finally, and called to the children, "Caleb, Ida Marie, come to the house now. We are going on a picnic, up to the old ruins."

The children came running laughing gleefully at the prospect of a picnic. Aida had promised them a picnic since they first arrived—and a trip to the ruins. Professor Custer had talked about the ruins a great deal and told them there was much to be learned there; he did not tell them the things they learned might be about themselves.

When, finally, they were ready and loaded in Aida's pickup truck, they made their way to the ranch's far canyon rim. The rutted track had been made by her grandfather to take rickety wagonloads of salt blocks to the high meadows. She remembered her grandfather as a no-nonsense sort who grew up in that country and seemed more married to the land than Aida's grandmother, a distant and slightly cold woman who showed her granddaughter little affection.

Aida's grandfather had known a good bit about the Anasazi, the sort of knowledge that comes only from living on the same ground and eking out a fragile existence under the same harsh conditions. He had a feel for this country, and for the kind of people it took to survive there. Aida remembered going along to haul the salt to outlying bunches of cattle each spring. Always they would stop at the ruins, and her grandfather would show her through the many rooms and point out the little things he had discovered but left in place. Unlike many area ranchers, the Winters' family did not hoard artifacts in personal collections or sell them to the occasional dealers passing through. They left the things in situ, just as they were abandoned those many hundred years ago.

The ruins lay in an alcove under a sandstone overhang and was considered very well preserved, at least for that part of the country, where most had already been ransacked by the late eighteen hundreds.

Aida warned the children to keep close as they wandered through the small, connected rooms. She explained to them how, as the building grew, the dark and airless interior rooms were often filled with trash and the offal of daily living. Some even contained burials she said, causing the children to look askance at the walled up doors to the anti-chambers. The Anasazi did not fear their dead and preferred to keep them close. It was not uncommon for family members to be buried under the dirt floors of the very rooms in which the family lived. Often it would be an infant or young child they couldn't bear to be apart from, even in death.

Aida told the children, "There were young people here just like you. They played on these very terraces, and the girls learned the work of their mothers—how to make pottery and grind corn. The boys learned to craft small bows and arrows and boasted to one another how they would 'make meat.'" Here Aida looked at Caleb, who had grown round-eyed at the thought of bows and arrows and boys who hunted like men. "Boys just like you, Caleb, who brought in small game and were important to the survival of their people.

Caleb puffed up and declared, "Once, I brought in a rabbit and we had it for breakfast."

Ida Marie sniffed and said, "Everyone knows the dog caught that rabbit."

"Yes," Caleb retorted, "but that dog would have ate it, too, if I hadn't taken it away from him." He smiled at the thought. *Paul T'Sosi promised me a single shot .22 rifle next year. Then I will show her who can 'make meat' for the family. In the meantime, maybe I will ask Paul how to make one of these bow and arrows. Paul is very old, and he probably made one himself when he was a boy.*

As they came out on a little side terrace, Aida pointed to the *manos* and *metates*—the trough-like milling stones used to grind corn and other seeds into meal. Some of them still lay on their eroded adobe bases, angled slightly against the stone walls. Many *metates* weighed upwards of fifty pounds. No wonder they were still there after nearly a thousand years.

Aida told them, "It probably took several years to shape a suitable *metate* stone into the smooth, hard trough necessary to grind and retain meal."

While stone grinding allowed more nutrients to be extracted from the flinty Anasazi corn, a certain amount of grit was unavoidable in the process. George Custer had said the gritty meal quickly wore down teeth. Bad teeth were often the cause of malnutrition and eventual death in those times. The average lifespan was only in the mid-to-late thirties. A person in his fifties would have been considered quite old, and it was the rare individual that went much past that. Of course, the same could be said of most primitive societies—the high infant death toll always figured heavily into the average.

Aida paused in front of a particularly fine example of a *metate* and said to Ida Marie, "It was the lucky girl that inherited a *metate* like this one. Good ones were passed down from generation to generation until they were worn completely through. It must have been a sad day when the family *metate* finally had to be discarded."

Later in the central plaza, sitting on the low rock rim of the main kiva, Aida opened the food basket they had brought, and the children ate the food and drank from their water bottles and wondered at how easy their life was compared to the ancient children who had lived here long ago.

Dr. George Custer, in his survey, had noted this kiva was one of the best-preserved examples in the entire Four Corners as far as he knew, and he had taken great pains to reseal the entry hole in the clay-covered roof. Aida's grandfather had originally just laid large, flat slabs of rock over the entrance and told family members there were things inside that were best left alone.

George Custer, following his survey of the ruin, cautioned Aida to let no one disturb the structure until it could be professionally evaluated and certain tests and lab work done on the contents. When Aida pressed the professor as to what he had found he said, "I am working on a paper that will cover this in minute detail, and I will send you a copy before its publication."

At the time, Aida hung on the professor's every word and was inclined to follow his instructions to the letter. Through the intervening years, however, she often thought of having a look inside the kiva for herself, but each time thought better of the inclination fearing she might disturb something important. George Custer seemed to regard the contents of this kiva as significantly pertinent to his research.

Little did she know, that spring day, that she and the children were having their lunch atop one of the most horrific scenes in Anasazi history.

7

The Clan

Lucy Tallwoman called Sue Yazzie from Shiprock to say Thomas's Uncle John Nez, the newly elected tribal councilman from Navajo Mountain, had come for a visit. He had brought his white friend, Marrisa, with him, and the two were excited to see the new baby. Lucy's father, Paul T'Sosi, was with them, as well, and wanted Sue to know he had a gift for the infant. Being early in the day, they thought they might just drop by, if it was all right with her. Navajo who are family or even just friends seldom bother to notify beforehand when coming for a visit; it would often not be possible, in any case. Since they were already in town, Lucy Tallwoman, knowing Sue better than most, felt it might be appreciated if she called ahead.

When the visitors arrived, Aunt Annie Eagletree was in the front yard hanging some wash on Sue's lilac bushes. She told Sue it would make the laundry smell good. Sue was not sure how much Charlie would like to smell like lilacs, but it might be good for the baby's diapers. Like many in that country, Sue had a washer but no dryer.

"It is silly to pay good money for something the wind will do for free," Aunt Annie said, and Lucy Tallwoman agreed, as she, too, thought a dryer an unnecessary expense, even though she herself had neither.

Annie's husband, Clyde, was hoeing the garden. Annie told him she thought he might be hoeing up some of the seedlings along with the weeds and that maybe he should let her do it. Clyde's eyes were getting bad, yet he refused to wear his glasses, saying he saw fine without them. Everyone knew this was a lie but did not want to hurt the old man's feelings by telling him so. Fortunately, Clyde had not worked his way to the far end of the garden, where Sue had laid out a small section in the old "Three Sisters" way of planting. The individual mounds contained multiple grains of hard blue corn, surrounded by beans and squash seeds. The corn stalks grew the quickest and provided a stout support for the beans. The squash covered the ground around the corn stalks to help retain moisture. But the major advantage was each plant provided essential nutrients needed by the other. In this way the same plot could sometimes be used for a number of seasons without depleting the soil. It was a very old way of farming along the washes and seeps in that country.

The county extension agent thought the method old fashioned and touted the newer fertilizers and insecticides. Still, many people found these old ways worked just fine, just as it had for a thousand years.

Everyone shook hands all around. Older Navajo consider handshaking an indispensable social grace and engage in it at every opportunity. It is thought the habit was picked up during the old "treaty councils" with the whites. Later it became a universal gesture of goodwill among the people. The *Dinè* have always been receptive to the customs of others, should those customs seem sensible to them.

Everyone gathered under the new brush arbor Clyde was working on. Clyde was nothing, if not industrious, and kept constantly busy about the little place. The brush arbor was one of his better efforts, and he was quite proud of it, though the roof tended to sag toward the back. Uncle Johnny nudged Marissa and pointed with his lips for her to move her chair from beneath the suspect section.

Sue told them the baby would be awake soon "That baby is trying to catch up on his sleep now that Charlie's not checking his diaper every five minutes." In the meantime, she served them all soft drinks from her new refrigerator.

Lucy Tallwoman had brought along several cans of Spam and two loaves of white bread from town, and a favorite Navajo lunch was prepared on the spot. Like many another poor people, the Navajo got used to eating Spam during the Second World War when it became common in government commodity packages. It was now actually preferred—fried or right out of the can—over many other meat products, and might show up at breakfast, lunch, or dinner.

After the meal, Clyde insisted Paul see how the garden was coming along. Paul was delighted to hear that Sue had planted blue Indian corn in her "Three Sisters" patch and made a mental note to ask her to save some of the pollen for him. The old, original, heritage lines of Indian blue corn, were getting harder and harder to come by.

As they walked up the rows, Paul said, "I can tell you have put a lot of work into this garden. I'm sure Charlie will be glad to see it." He didn't bother to mention the little chopped-up corn stalks and pepper plants he saw lying among the hoed-up weeds.

Sue went to the house for more drinks but instead came back with the baby, who, still half asleep, looked blearily around the gathering. Marissa and Lucy immediately came forward to hold the child.

"What is this baby's name?" Marrisa asked the baby in a playful voice, taking him from his mother's arms.

Sue could not keep the pride from her voice as she replied for everyone to hear, "His Navajo name is *Ashkii Ana'dlohi.*"

"Wait," Marissa cried, "don't tell me. Let me guess what it could mean in English!" Marissa was an anthropologist who came to Navajo Mountain to work on her thesis concerning the juxtaposition between the Navajo language and that of their Athabaskan cousins in the far

Northwest. Her studies focused mainly on the words Navajo women might use, which are sometimes different from what men would say in a similar situation.

In the course of her work, Marissa and Thomas Begay's uncle, John Nez, had met at a chapter house meeting and over time became a couple and, in fact, now lived together—causing a certain amount of speculation on that part of the reservation.

"I've got it," Marissa grinned finally. "His name is Laughing Boy!"

Lucy Tallwoman looked at Sue and clapped her hands. "I have not heard that name in a long time *Chih keh*. Where did you come up with that?"

"It was Charlie's idea. He said, in school, Professor Custer suggested he read *Laughing Boy* by Oliver LaFarge. It is still his favorite Navajo book. He made me read it too, and I liked that name as much as him."

"I always loved that book." Marrisa smiled. "It will be a lucky name for this little baby."

The baby, with his shoe button-eyes and unruly shock of black hair, only grimaced, the only one not to laugh.

When old Paul T'Sosi followed Clyde back from the garden and was informed of the baby's name, he beamed, "That was my Grandfather's name when he was little." His gaze lingered on his daughter Lucy, who was now holding the baby, "He was a good man. It was said everyone liked him. That was back in the time when men were still weavers, too. He taught my grandmother how to make blankets, and she taught Lucy's mother." Paul had to look away for a moment, "It is a fine name. He will someday make everyone proud." Paul was careful not to actually say the name of his grandfather, as it was not thought right to refer to the dead, even by their boyhood name. But when he came up and shook the baby's fat little hand, he said, *"Ah-hah-lah'nih Ashkii Ana'dlohi,"* using the affectionate greeting of the Dinè, and once again knowing the taste of his grandfather's name on his tongue.

Lucy passed the baby back to Sue, while Paul dug in his Levi's pocket for a small goatskin bag on a leather thong. "Hang this above his crib. It will be his medicine bag for now and will help protect him from things he cannot yet know." Paul waved the bag over the infant's head. "Later he can add his own sacred things, and its power will grow." Here he paused and with a stern eye, warned, "He must never show the contents of this bag to any other person."

Sue took the bag and in a whisper thanked Paul T'Sosi for the gift and for his prayers at the hospital. She somehow felt certain this old man had helped her son through a very dangerous time.

8

The Fight

George Custer's camp fell into quite a tizzy when they arrived for their morning's work and discovered someone had once again violated the dig. Harley Ponyboy reached the site first, hoping to get his choice of the shovels, few of which suited his short arms. He reported the news at the top of his lungs but forgot to speak English and was not understood—except by Charlie Yazzie and Thomas Begay, who ran the rest of the way up the hill.

"That's it," Thomas declared surveying the damage. "I've had it with these people coming in here in the night and tearing stuff up." And things were torn up: grid stakes again pulled out, carefully arranged potsherds waiting to be catalogued, now strewn about the ground; and a section of wall was pushed over into an adjoining trench, damaging a delicate collage of woven material.

Professor Custer arrived last and was outraged, his usual calm demeanor disappearing as he addressed the group. "Rather than just acts of random vandalism, what we have here is a malicious and deliberate attempt to thwart our work; one we can no longer ignore." He shaded his brow with a trembling hand and glared off into the canyons to the east. He then turned and addressed the three Dinè, "Charlie, I think you men should get started now instead of tomorrow as we had planned."

Charlie nodded. "The sign can't be over a few hours old and it appears there was only one person involved this time. He shouldn't be too hard to follow." He looked at his two companions and waved a hand toward his vehicle. "We had better swing by the truck and pick up a few things, we may not make it back tonight." Thomas, smiling, instantly took this to mean they would retrieve Charlie's .38 from the glove box of the locked truck.

The woman in charge of the mess crew called to Harley that he should stop by the cook tent for sandwiches, and George Custer moved closer to Charlie and said quietly, "Don't take any unnecessary risks out there. Should you find a camp, just report back, and we'll send for the tribal police."

Charlie nodded but reminded the professor it might require a long drive out of the canyon just to make radio contact with the authorities. "George, there is a chance we may have to deal with this ourselves. We'll just have to see how it plays out."

The professor reluctantly agreed but cautioned, "At least send for help if you think it's something bigger than you three can handle"

Tanya Griggs, from her assigned work space at the side of an upper wall, watched through lidded eyes as the three Navajo left camp, each with a small rucksack, apparently determined to stay out until they found some answers. She hoped they didn't find more than they bargained for.

~~~~~~~

Circling the far perimeter of the camp, it didn't take Harley Ponyboy long to pick up a single set of tracks with a Caterpillar imprint. "Looks like he's headed off towards the big canyon." He canted his head in thought. "An he don't seem ta care who knows it, neither."

Charlie studied the tracks for a moment, and then indicated with his chin for Thomas Begay to have a look. "It's the big guy again."

After examining the tracks, Thomas said, "It's hard to believe one person could do all that damage, but these tracks were the only odd ones we could identify at the dig." He rubbed his chin. "I think this big boy is the only one of the outlaws still in the area—same tracks Harley found near the trucks, too."

Charlie nodded. "Yes, and I think he might have been the one skulking around behind the professor's tent the night I got here, too. Those two people that were involved the first time haven't been back, from what I've seen, but this big one has stuck around." His face turned grim as he swung his head in the direction of the canyon. "If there is a camp, it belongs to this big man."

On the trail, Harley Ponyboy set a pace somewhere between a running walk and a jog trot and, after an hour, it had taken its toll. Thomas leaned up against a tree to catch his breath. Charlie, too, was clearly winded but had refused to slack off the pace. He leaned over, hands on knees, and drew in huge gulps of air.

Thomas wheezed as he waved a dismissive arm at Charlie. "I think you better take a break," he choked. "You're out of shape, college boy." He then went down on one knee, coughed up phlegm and spat it on the ground. When finally he had regained the power of speech, he shook his head at Charlie and said in a hoarse whisper, "It's embarrassing to see you like this."

Only short, round, little Harley Ponyboy seemed unfazed by the morning's punishing pace. "Didn' you two never run ta meet the dawn when you were lit'le boys?" Harley grinned at them. "My uncle used ta come before daylight and throw cold water on my brother and me and say, 'If you boys don't run to meet the sun, he will not smile on you today.'"

In earlier times Indian boys were generally taught by uncles, their fathers being considered too easy on them, causing boys to grow soft and weak. An uncle was generally not so emotionally invested and would provide the tough love the boys needed to grow, physically and mentally; many Indian tribes held this same belief.

The tracks were fresh but kept to hard and rocky ground. A lesser tracker than Harley might have lost them completely. It was several more miles to the east before the dwindling sign turned and headed for the canyon rim then disappeared completely as they hit slick rock.

It was beginning to cloud up again, as a fresh breeze welled up out of the canyon and gushed over the rim, causing the gnarly, little piñon trees to sigh and sway. It was exactly the sort of breeze a hunter would want in his face.

Harley Ponyboy, still in the lead, quietly held up a hand and motioned for the others to stay and remain silent. He then eased off into a patch of oak brush that ran down a rocky gully to the rim and an overlook.

Charlie and Thomas, eyes slitted against the wind, waited impatiently, and did not hear the big man come up behind them. He was nearly upon them when some sixth sense caused Thomas to turn.

Thomas Begay had been hit some awful blows in his life, but nothing like the fist the size of a small ham that now sent him sprawling backward and right into Charlie Yazzie—who reeled, hands clawing the air, before he too went down flat on his back. Charlie's eyes widened as he looked into the leering face of a man even he thought could be a "bigfoot."

"Whatchu little men do'n' out here so far from the Dinè Bikeyah?" The apparition grinned through yellowed and uneven teeth. He leveled a short-barreled pump shotgun at them, "You're on the 'Uta' reservation now… trespassers!" There was something almost wild in the man's demeanor, and something else Charlie couldn't quite put a finger on. The man tilted his head from side to side, as though listening to something only he could hear. There was a slight tick in his left eye.

Thomas, apparently out cold, or possibly even dead, lay absolutely still. The astute observer, however, might have noticed a slight movement of his right hand, which was partially hidden beneath him.

Thomas Begay had thought he should be the one to carry the .38 this time. He well knew Charlie's reticence when it came to shooting people—a trait he felt had nearly gotten them both killed a time or two. The Smith & Wesson was now in his waistband under his shirt, his gun hand already on the grip.

All Charlie could think of was what his Aunt Annie Eagletree said about patterning a shotgun's pellets. This particular shotgun should throw a rather wide pattern, in his opinion. Their only hope at this point seemed to lie with Harley Ponyboy, whom this person might still be unaware of. The thought had no more than crossed his mind when the big man whispered, "Where's you fat little friend?" He looked past Charlie toward the canyon rim. "That boy's a good tracker, but he shoulda seen I was making it too easy for him." He almost smiled. "That is a very old Ute trick, and you are not the first Dinè to fall for it."

Charlie's mind fell into that calm, autonomous drift the mind reserves for periods of deep distress. He gave absolutely no outward sign as he watched Harley Ponyboy ease up behind the brutish hulk, a rock the size of a baseball at the end of his throwing arm. It was at this moment Thomas Begay stirred slightly and moaned as he rolled to his side, causing the big man to swing the shotgun to cover him.

The smooth, round rock caught the big Ute full force at the base of his skull, and he rocked back on his heels. His eyes rolled slightly upward in his head, but he did not go down, only blinked several times, as though gathering his wits.

Thomas, still groggy, but fast regaining his faculties, came to his knees, revolver in hand, hammer back. He saw instantly that Harley's rock was not enough and squeezed off a shot that smashed through the Ute's great paw, shattering both the hand and the shotgun's stock.

Harley, never faint of spirit when it came to a fight, rushed the big man, tackling him, bringing him to one knee. This broke the Ute's grip on what was left of the shotgun and sent it skittering across the sandstone shelf.

The Ute roared as he came to his senses and backhanded Harley with the bloody wreck of his right hand, causing him such exquisite pain he shrieked in agony, a terrifying scream like that of a woman or cougar. This so unnerved Thomas Begay he began wildly flinging lead—sending all four remaining shots wide of their mark.

The huge Ute came instantly to his feet and leaped beyond the reach of his tormentors and in only a few bounds was at the canyon edge and gone.

Charlie, frozen in place at this nearly instantaneous chain of events, looked to see how Harley fared. The little man's face was covered with blood, both his and that of the wounded Ute. He regarded Charlie with a gap-toothed grin. "That was an old Navajo trick the Utes never knowed about." Harley fished around inside his jaw with his tongue and retrieved a missing tooth. Holding it carefully by the enamel portion, he reinserted it in the socket and pushed it down firmly enough to seat it. "Sometimes tis works if you get it back in quick enough." He grinned again to show the results of his work. He was lucky the tooth had been tight with its brothers and could be wedged into place. This was not Harley's first rodeo.

Charlie grimaced and pushed his tongue against his own front teeth as he tilted his head at Harley's newly replanted tooth. *That had to hurt. Harley was a tough little booger. You had to give him that.*

Despite being battered and shaken, the three Dinè fell into pursuit of the wounded Ute and worked their way along the crevasse leading into the canyon. Harley reached down and retrieved the shotgun as they passed through the crevasse, "I wish't I had me some Duck Tape," he lisped, trying to keep his tongue away from the newly planted tooth. "I think maybe I could fix tis ting."

Thomas frowned, "That would be good, Harley, cause I'm out of bullets."

"That's okay. I can still make this scattergun shoot if we need it." Harley knew he could fire the gun using just the pistol grip, should it come to that.

At the truck, Thomas had taken Charlie seriously when he said, "Anyone who needs more than five rounds is either incompetent or reckless." This was more of Aunt Annie Eagletree's wisdom. Charlie thought it sounded like something Clint Eastwood might say in a "Dirty Harry" movie and had remembered it. Thomas, not wanting to be thought incompetent, or reckless, had left the full box of extra ammunition in the glove compartment.

Harley was once again in front and followed the spatters of blood—hard to see on the red rock. Thomas, in the rear, kept an eagle eye on their back trail. He wasn't sure what the Ute was capable of now. It wasn't unthinkable that this person was a shape-shifter, or worse.

Charlie cautioned both men to watch their step as the old Anasazi trail now clung precariously to the side of the cliff. One misstep could prove fatal. Blood still flecked the rocky trail ahead, telling Harley Ponyboy the Ute was indeed still in front of them, where he belonged.

Thomas turned his full attention to the path ahead and whispered loudly to be heard above the wind, "Charlie, who did that Ute remind you of?"

Without thinking, Charlie replied, "Hiram Buck." *That was exactly what had been bothering him about the Ute all along, right down to the twitch in the left eye.* "But Hiram Buck's dead and gone, Hastiin."

"Yes," Thomas raised his voice above a particularly strong gust, "but his younger brother, Ira Buck, isn't dead.

Hiram ran him off years ago. People thought he was afraid Ira would want a split of the inheritance." After a pause, he went on, "Last I heard he was living in Cortez—a derrick hand on a work-over rig. He wasn't there long until the tool-pusher was found dead under the platform one morning with his head banged in. It was rumored Ira let a chain get loose on purpose. That's not unheard of on a rig in this country. It was well known the two didn't get along; but no one was charged. The other 'hands' said they were in the doghouse at the time and claimed they hadn't seen anything—too scared to come forward, I guess." Thomas paused and flattened himself against the cliff and edged along a particularly thin section of trail. He had been so involved in his talk he had nearly failed to follow Charlie's lead. "Ira sort of disappeared after that. I had forgotten all about him myself. Sally Klee used to say he was bigger than his brother, but not as smart. She said he would never mess with Hiram, though. As head of the clan, Hiram could have killed Ira if he got in his way, and Ira knew it."

This was a development Charlie was not happy with. *If this was Ira Buck and he was as crazy as Hiram--or George Jim, even—he was capable of anything. But then this Ute had already made it clear what he was capable of.*

Harley stopped abruptly and motioned them back as gravel sifted down off a high ledge, followed by heavy rock and debris—a slide that totally blocked the trail.

Harley peered through clouds of choking red dust and knew they would not be going farther that day. "By the time we find another way down, that bad boy will be long gone." He looked up to where a huge slab of rock had been pulled loose. "He's purty smart for a big, dumb bastard."

"We won't catch him today." Charlie agreed. "But I bet we haven't seen the last of him, either."

Thomas only grunted and rubbed his jaw, which had continued to swell, making his face look lopsided. Under his breath he said, "I hope we do meet him again."

~~~~~~~~

The next day, when Charlie made his report to George Custer, it was clear he thought they were safe, for the present at least. "It will take that Ute a while to get over the shattered hand, if he ever does get over it."

"Maybe," the professor replied, "but we still can't rule out those other two coming back. I think we better post a night guard up at the site." He hesitated, and then said, "Charlie, I think there's another thing you should know. Ira Buck was one of the hired hands on the survey at Aida Winters' ranch. Tanya Griggs's mother, Myra, and he were pretty friendly." The professor hesitated. "More than friends, some thought, though it's hard to imagine."

Charlie took a moment to digest this and then nodded. "That's starting to make a little more sense. That would explain the connection between these people, and why they are working together. Myra and her husband Steven are not anxious to see your research go forward, or for your new paper to be published."

"No, they aren't. One reason being the Hopi's strong claims to Anasazi heritage. Some think it's why they fought so hard for the Native American Graves Protection and Reparations Act. They needed to show cause for an expansion of their reservation borders toward their sacred homeland. That proposed expansion included water and grazing rights worth millions."

Here, Charlie held up a finger. "George, that theory has been worked to death. And while it may justify their never-ending dispute with the Navajo Nation, it's been a stretch trying to validate that line of reasoning in a court of law—at least it has been so far."

Privately, Charlie couldn't help but commiserate with his former professor. The Reparations Act had been a crushing blow for archaeology and its related institutions, including museums and university research facilities. It interrupted vital research-in-progress and gutted important museums of their most enthralling displays; their traffic was affected to the point some of them still struggled financially.

The professor waved away Charlie's argument and, as though reading his thoughts, concluded, "The removal of the burial remains, and funerary material from museums was a colossal loss. More importantly, Americans, including the very tribes involved, lost a vital link to those people—destroying a near palpable bond with an entire culture—one that cannot be replaced with dioramas and pottery displays. The public has forever lost the essence of those ancient people." George Custer paused, breathless, and threw up his hands. "It was all gone with one legislative swipe of a pen." He lowered his eyes and shook his head. "All gone."

A good portion of George Custer's life had been spent in the research and study of those very collections, many of which he himself contributed to. Charlie could understand what must be going through his mind, remembering those years of hard work. While everything in those collections had been documented, cataloged, and photographed, it did not mitigate the fact that latter technology might contribute new and exciting knowledge, some never before dreamed possible.

"So," Charlie asked, "you're thinking the daughter, Tanya Griggs, played a part in these attacks we've had here?"

"Well, it would make sense, I suppose." The professor waved his pencil in the air. "I know it's a serious accusation. She seems innocent enough, and no one so far has reported anything that would implicate her in any way." He laid the pencil down and admitted, "We could be barking up the wrong tree entirely, of course, but we need to find some way to verify her involvement, one way or the other. Indeed, there may not have been any involvement at all."

Charlie went away from the meeting still uncertain in the matter of Tanya Griggs. *But why else would this Hopi girl have applied for the expedition except to help her mother and father stop George Custer's research?* As he made his way over to the mess tent to join Harley and Thomas, he was determined to find some way to prove or disprove the complicity of Tanya Griggs.

It was nearly noon; his two friends already in the mess tent were the center of attention, and had attracted several sympathetic onlookers. Some were aghast at Thomas's swollen features and the reconstructed tooth Harley so proudly displayed was the object of much interest.

One expedition member, Bob Mills, who had been a dental student before switching his field of study to dental forensics, had Harley open wide and then carefully examined the tooth using a teaspoon for a tongue depressor. "I don't see why that won't work out for you, Harley. From what you say, it was never out of your mouth and was reinserted soon enough to insure a live root. There was little I could have done differently to save it."

Harley grinned at this and called to Charlie, "The tooth. Doc says I did good." He turned back to the dentist. "This is the second tooth I lost this way, and that other one is just fine now. Maybe I should have been a dentist."

The dental expert chuckled and clapped Harley on the shoulder. "You probably would have made a good one, Harley, and maybe not have gotten these teeth knocked out to start with."

Tanya Griggs had not gathered around with the others and now stood quietly near the stove tending a large pot— only occasionally glancing their way. She was uncertain what to make of these latest developments and wondered at the curious stares of these three Navajo.

Thomas was surprised when he heard George Custer's information regarding Tanya Griggs. He sighed. "Well, that's a damn shame. She's a good worker, and everyone seems to like her, too."

Charlie was adamant. "We'd best keep an eye on her, she may well be tied in with all this." As he said this he caught the girl's eye and quickly looked away. "No one has proof of any wrongdoing—not yet, anyway." Charlie didn't like the idea any better than Thomas.

After the crowd of Harley Ponyboy's admirers dissipated and the three were free to talk, Harley, too, was updated regarding Tanya Griggs, which caused him to say, "Hmmph." In such a way Charlie took to mean there was some serious doubt in his mind. "She might be a part of something but maybe not in the way you think. When her and me was working together up in the trench she said she could not wait ta see what was in the kiva. Sounded ta me like she don't have no clue what's in there."

"Do *you* have any clue what's in there Harley?" Charlie wanted to know.

"More than you maybe think, Charlie." The little man looked guardedly around the tent. "When the professor and me was drink'n', he tol' me a lot of things about that kiva." Harley nodded wisely. "He read me his paper one night too. I didn' really understand a lot of it, but I got a good idea what the professor is looking for."

Thomas gave Harley Ponyboy a suspicious stare. "What's that Harley?

Harley stared right back and said, "I can't tell you. The professor said if I tol' anyone, he would have to kill me."

Charlie and Thomas exchanged smiles and Thomas asked, "Do you really think Professor Custer would kill you Harley?"

"From some of the things he said, I would not doubt it." Again Harley looked around the tent and whispered,

"Once down in..." He stopped himself. "I tol' you guys I couldn' tell you! Now don't ask no more."

Charlie and Thomas eyed one another again, but this time they didn't smile.

That night Thomas propped up the side of the cook tent with a little forked stick. From his sleeping mat there was a clear view of the women's tent across the way. One way or the other, he intended to watch Tanya Griggs a little more closely from now on. Harley snored peacefully next to him, and Thomas once again thought it strange Harley Ponyboy should be in the confidence of Professor George Custer. Thomas had been keeping a close eye out for any drinking on the professor's part but so far had not seen any evidence of it. Charlie told him that it was nearly impossible to tell when the professor was drinking until he crossed over that invisible line. *What invisible line? Who knew where that line was?* Thomas knew one thing for certain *it was a different line for an Irishman than it was for an Indian.*

~~~~~~~

For the next several days, George Custer's crew settled into an industrious routine that caused the expedition's progress to advance at a steady rate. The professor now thought it certain this site was indeed a reconstruction of an older village. This particular transitory group of Anasazi would have lived here in the exact middle of the great migration period. His senior crewmembers were of one mind—the last residents of this village had probably lived here no more than twenty, or thirty years total before worsening conditions forced them to move on. But thirty years was a long time in those days—a lifetime for many.

As the expedition's crew gathered for lunch in the shade of the overhang, Professor Custer attempted to explain to those team members from other areas, some of the environmental nuances affecting these particular prehistoric people.

"The uninitiated, looking at the huge and complex building done by the Anasazi," Custer began, "tend to think the original builders inhabited these great stone structures for many hundreds of years at a stretch.

"The fact is many of these settlements were only occupied from thirty to fifty years at a time, though a few exceptionally well-endowed locations did continue in use for longer periods." He paused for effect. "There was good reason for these short-term occupations. Chief among them was the depletion of natural resources in the area— dwindling supplies of firewood, big game, and the exhaustion of prime farm ground. Periodic but localized droughts, in varying degrees of intensity, affected springs and streams in these isolated areas, making these settlements untenable for long periods. The failure of a single local water supply might provoke moves of many miles." He looked around the group and invited comment.

The graduate student from Colombia raised her hand and said, "At home my work is centered around the lowlands, where lack of water was never a problem and those sites were sometimes occupied for centuries."

"Yes," the professor agreed, "that is true, but here finding unsettled areas with fresh resources was much more problematic, and it became more and more difficult to satisfy the Anasazi's increasing numbers.

"Every few decades, regional dry periods of indeterminate length caused entire populations to change location, sometimes involving long distances. Of course, a band of people might only move to an area that had been previously occupied but had lain fallow for many years. Over time these abandoned areas often regenerated and once again were capable of sustaining a new population."

Custer stopped to gauge his audience's interest and finding it sufficient to continue, had a sip of water from his canteen and went on. "Between 700 and 1130 a particularly benign weather pattern set in over the Four Corners area, allowing the growing Anasazi population to flourish as never before. Precipitation increased and crop yields became more generous. Snowmelt kept streams flowing beyond anything previously known, and additional ground water allowed the expansion of dry-land farming on the mesa tops.

"This period later became the "Golden Age" of the Anasazi—the very peak of their civilization." Here the professor's voice became bleak. "Unfortunately, this more stable interlude was followed by the gradual advancement of one of the great droughts of the preceding thousand years. Finally, such a severe and generalized dry period ensued as to inflict great suffering upon these hardy people. Water diversion and cofferdams, even irrigation canals, were built throughout the region but, in the end, even that didn't help."

At this point, a rather sad look crossed Dr. Custer's face and he lowered his eyes in thought. "Eventually, dry-land fields began to disappear, forcing people to move to the deeper canyons for a more dependable source of water and to escape a more urgent threat, internecine warfare—groups of their own or very similar people turning against one another in this time of starvation. A culture of coexistence had flourished among the Anasazi of the Colorado plateau for a very long time. But, as in every age and land, desperate people tend to engage in desperate practices—one of these is war; the other is religion."

Harley Ponyboy surprised everyone by holding up his hand and, when called on asked, "Dr. Custer, did we Navajo have anything to do with these Indians disappearing? I've heard some people say that we may have run them off."

George smiled and said, "Harley, some early authorities used to think that, but later research has pretty much proven the Anasazi were already gone by the time the Athabaskan people moved down from the North."

The professor nodded approvingly in Harley's direction and continued his talk. "As the years of famine continued and prayers to the rain-gods went unanswered, we suspect the people began casting about for a new and more powerful conduit to their deities. Strong influences from Mexico were filtering into the Chaco Canyon complex and spreading North like wildfire. One of these was the *Kachina* phenomenon. It was probably during this time that there developed a growing separation between the have and have-nots—those with food, and those without. It may have started with the outliers, the small bands in the hinterlands, who maintained only sporadic contact with the large villages. The drought would have hit them especially hard. And as these people became bolder, more desperate, they may have become more determined in their depredations on their more fortunate brethren, people who might still have had food for *their* children."

The veteran members of the crew, already familiar with Dr. Custer's theories, had begun drifting back to work, when a shout arose from the main kiva excavation.

Charlie Yazzie, who was first to arrive, was already down in the kiva when Professor Custer hurried up and ordered several others back from the partially collapsed west wall. Dust rose in a haze nearly obscuring Tanya Griggs, who lay covered in rock and dirt.

"Is she all right?" Professor Custer called to Charlie who was now bending over the young woman.

"I can't tell, doc. Looks like she's out." Charlie was of a mind to pull her out from under the fallen rock when someone bumped into him from behind.

One of the team slid down the embankment despite the professor's warning and carefully began to clear debris from the girl.

It was the Cherokee undergrad from Oklahoma, Ted Altman. "I'm an EMT," he said quietly and took over. "Let's not lift her until we have a better idea of her injuries."

That made sense to Charlie, who could see this was clearly someone who knew what he was doing. "Whatever you say. How can I help?"

"Just give me a minute to do a quick check and then maybe we can get her out of here."

It was an unusually large kiva, not as large as the Great Kiva at Aztec, but certainly one of the larger ones Charlie had seen. The room had been rebuilt from an older burned-out structure, and the refurbishment had been shoddily done, a fact pointed out by Professor Custer at the beginning of the excavation.

"Her pulse is good and her pupils look okay, too," the EMT turned archaeologist announced. "Arms and legs seem alright as well. I think we can move her out of here if we are careful."

The professor now signaled two more of the onlookers into the pit, and the four people supported the stricken woman and passed her up above their heads to others anxious to help. Among these were Harley Ponyboy and Thomas Begay. Charlie and Thomas exchanged glances as the girl was passed up, and Thomas could see more than concern for the girl in his expression and made a mental note to find out later what that was about.

Tanya Griggs was conscious by the time she was taken to her tent, where she was closely attended by the expeditions other two female members. After a more thorough examination, EMT Ted Altman, pronounced her very lucky indeed. He could find no major contusion or injury, remarkable considering the amount of material they had cleared off of her.

When Professor Custer came to visit the injured girl that afternoon, he was not surprised to find Ted Altman by her bedside. The young undergrad quickly excused himself, and the professor, after inquiring how Tanya felt, made some small comment regarding how lucky they were to have Ted in the group and saw the girl attempt a smile.

The Professor cleared his throat and asked, not unkindly, "Tanya, what were you doing in the kiva? I've made it quite clear the kiva was only to be entered during work hours and with the assigned group." Before the girl could answer, his tone became slightly stern. "This might be a good time to ask why you applied for this program in the first place?"

Tanya half raised from her pillows and protested. "Dr. Custer...."

The professor, however, did not let her finish before saying, "Tanya, I'm well aware there are people who do not want this project to move forward—people that are very close to you. You are a talented young woman with a true passion for your work and a promising career ahead of you. I would hate to see misplaced trust, someone else's vendetta, for lack of a better word, impact that future." The professor sat back and watched closely as Tanya Griggs considered what he had said. Her eyes never left his and there was something there, something the professor had not noticed in the girl before. Not defiance; more like a force of independent spirit, and one not easily quelled.

The girl sat straight up, though the effort caused a catch in her breath and a fleeting grimace of pain. "I am not my mother, or my father!" As she twisted the sheet in her hands, she hoarsely whispered, "I have seen my parents torn apart by this since I was young. They are scientists, tortured by the need to do what's right in regard to their profession and, at the same time, for the Hopi people." She paused a moment. "My father has gone along with my mother's concept of what's right for the Hopi. I sometimes have the impression that concept is not grounded in truth." She looked away and seemed to lose her train of thought.

Professor Custer regarded the girl carefully before asking, and more gently, "Have you had any contact with your parents while you were here?"

Tanya looked him straight in the eye and said, "No, I have not."

George Custer gave her a long, searching look and reached in his shirt pocket for the small beaded amulet Thomas had found when tracking the first intruders. "Do you recognize this?"

Tanya took the beadwork and turned it over, examining both the leather backing and beadwork front. "Yes, I recognize it. I made it. My mother and I beaded these moccasin pulls for one another last Christmas." She looked to her corner of the tent where her tall knee-length moccasins stood.

The professor followed her gaze. "I noticed the Zia Sun emblem pulls on your moccasins the first night you were here." George Custer was suddenly struck by the fact that mother and daughter had made exactly contradictory designs for each other's moccasin-pulls—one the Sun symbol and the other the Hopi Rain symbol. One did not have to be a psychologist to read meaning into this.

George Custer stood to go. "Tanya, ordinarily I would send you packing but, in this case, the logistics of the thing would only further detract from our work here. You think it over, and if you do want to go home, the boys are going in for supplies tomorrow and can put you on a bus in Cortez."

As he turned to leave, a soft voice behind him said, "There is an old Hopi saying; 'All dreams fall from the same sky.'"

Charlie was waiting outside the tent for the professor and fell in with him as they headed back up to the dig. "I couldn't help but hear most of that. What do you think?"

"She seemed sincere, like she intended coming to her own conclusions about our work here. Maybe that's what she was doing in the kiva. The same thing we are all doing, really—trying to get at the truth." Then after a bit of thought he went on, "I actually don't know quite what to think." The professor sounded tired. "I wish I had a drink."

"Why don't you have one then? I suspected you might have a bottle hid out." Charlie grinned when he said this but was serious at the same time.

"I did have a bottle—in that hollow log by my tent. I smashed it the second night we were here." He chuckled. "I figured you boys were on to me."

Charlie laughed and gave the professor a pat on the back. "Harley stuck up for you but did allow you might keep a bottle for snakebite and such. He said you might have trouble finding enough snakes, though."

The Professor nodded, smiled, and changed the subject. "When you and the boys go into town tomorrow there's something I'd like for you to do for me."

9

The Snake

On the drive out the next morning, the Chevy Suburban had nearly reached the highway when they came upon a band of sheep being herded by an old man on a horse, helped by two scruffy dogs. The dogs flanked the sheep, and the man brought up the drag. He neither acknowledged the vehicle nor slowed his pace. When just abreast of him, Charlie let the truck idle alongside.

Thomas hailed him in the usual fashion, "Yaa' eh t'eeh," and then asked in Navajo, "Where to, Uncle?"

The man had his neckerchief across his face leaving only his eyes exposed to the dust. He didn't answer immediately but persuaded his horse to pick a way through the sheep and even closer to the truck. Once alongside, Thomas could see he was much older than he first thought. The old man returned the greeting and added, "That is a fine car you have there, Grandson... you didn't steal it, I hope."

Thomas indicated the two white people in the back seat with his chin. "Oh no, Grandfather," he said, switching to the more respectful term *Acheii*. "We have only just kidnapped these white people and are taking their car for a little ride."

The old man smiled and nodded "Well, you picked a nice day for it, if no one catches you."

The two bantered back and forth in the old way of the Dinè, when people made time for such things. Charlie kept his eyes on his driving and the sheep. He let on like he didn't understand the conversation between Thomas and the old man, which was partially true.

"What will you trade me for this car, Grandfather?" Thomas demanded of the old man. "That is a fine horse you are riding. What would you have to have for him?"

"Oh, I couldn't part with this horse, Grandson, I have had him since I was a little boy, and it makes me sad to think of selling him." He reached down and rubbed the horse on the neck. "You are the second person in two days who has wanted this horse." He shook his head. "I didn't know old horses were in such demand these days. Anyway, you would have to be a pretty good cowboy to ride him. He is not the kind of horse just anyone can ride."

This made Thomas smile—he liked this old man.

The two white people in the back seat of the Suburban didn't understand Navajo. The anthropologist from WNMU would like to have known what the two were saying, but she thought it best not to ask. Her young undergrad companion silently agreed and looked away when the old man fell back a few feet and peered into the side window at them. When he caught back up, the old man said. "Those white people do not look too happy Grandson. Have you treated them badly?"

"Nothing beyond what they deserved Grandfather."

Usually, only the old people still joked like this, and the old man was pleased to hear it from someone younger. He looked more closely at Thomas and speculated. "Those white people must have put up a pretty good fight to give you such a lump on the jaw."

Thomas touched his jaw and with a frown said, "Oh, no, Grandfather, these whites have been no trouble at all. They are frightened of wild Indians and leave us to our business." He stuck his jaw out, so the old man might better grasp the gravity of the protuberance on his face. "I got this lump from a giant Ute down in the canyons." Thomas eyed the old man. "Have you seen such a person in your travels, Grandfather?"

The old man shot Thomas a sharp glance and jerked his horse closer to the truck. "Did that Ute have a bad hand?" He held up one hand and let it dangle from his wrist. "If that is the same Ute, you did well to get away with only a broken jaw."

Thomas glanced across at Charlie and raised an eyebrow, then, turning back to the old man said quietly, "Yes, that is the one. He gave me this jaw, and I repaid him with that useless hand. I expect I will get over this jaw before he gets over the hand. I always try to repay what I owe, Grandfather—good or bad."

The old man nodded and replied, "That is good. That is the way it used to be with men in this country."

Thomas waited patiently for the old man to continue.

"Yes, I have seen him, just the other night in the big canyon they call 'Splits In Two.' He came by my camp just as I was having my dinner. I didn't like the look of him, but I invited him to eat, as any person with manners might do. It was only a rabbit roasted on a stick, but he seemed satisfied to eat a good bit of it." The old man reined his horse so close it almost touched the truck and lowered his voice. "When the rabbit was gone, he asked if he could borrow my horse, as he needed to get to town and see a doctor." And here the old fellow paused, as though remembering exactly how the thing had happened. "I told him I was sorry to say it, but I needed this horse to get my sheep home and I could not let him have it." The old man cocked his head "That is when he grew angry and said he might just take the horse anyway. He did not see that I had my 30-30 just under my blanket. When I let it show, he could see I meant business. He cursed then and went straight away down the canyon. When he was well out of sight I moved my blankets back into the trees, behind some rocks. I did not sleep well that night, Grandson. I waited for him, but he did not come back."

"It was good you had that gun with you Grandfather. That was a bad man you shared rabbit with that night."

The old fellow only nodded, and having told all he knew, abruptly turned his horse away and only waved in parting.

Thomas called after him, "If you should see that Ute again, *Acheii* we would take it as a favor if you would let us know," and then shouted as the old man drew farther away, "We are at the Anasazi ruin up Left Hand Canyon."

The old man again waved an arm and called to his dogs that had been resting in the shade.

The sheep gave way for the big Suburban as an ocean gives way to a ship—filling in behind like a foaming white sea of wool.

~~~~~~~~~

In downtown Cortez, Charlie dropped off the two crewmembers and their supply list, saying he should be back by three o'clock and would pick them up in front of the supermarket. He cautioned them to have the store people throw some wrapped dry ice in with the fresh meat and to pack everything to survive a rough trip back in.

Harley pointed out a bar they should stay clear of. "Those people in there don't take ta strangers very well. I expect you would be better off not going in there." The little man noticed Thomas eyeing the bar and recalled when his friend had once become involved in an altercation with a Jicarilla Apache. At the time, Thomas had not thought himself drunk enough to make a good fight of it, and proceeded to just talk the Apache into submission. The Jicarilla, not able to get a word in edgewise, finally threw up his hands in frustration. "You could talk a turkey down from his tree," he said, and walked away in disgust. Thomas often talked himself out of bad situations, something Harley had never been very good at. This was

Thomas's great charm; Harley thought, *he could talk a fencepost into line, should he take a notion.*

Thomas leaned out the passenger-side window and looked longingly at the bar as they passed. He and Harley had spent some happy times in that bar, but secretly he knew you had to enjoy a good fight to make the most of the experience.

Charlie turned to the other two. "We have to make a quick stop to pick up something for the professor, and I have a couple of phone calls to make. Then we can head out to Aida Winters' place and see the kids." He knew this was the main reason Thomas had come along in the first place.

When Charlie came out of the florists with a huge bouquet, he pulled out the letter the professor had given him to deliver along with the flowers and stared thoughtfully at it.

Harley Ponyboy raised his eyebrows twice in quick succession at the flowers and asked slyly, "Are those for me?"

Thomas burst out laughing.

Charlie thrust the flowers at the little man and said, "No, but you can hold them until we get to the ranch."

As they pulled through the ranch gate, they spotted Aida Winters and the children down at the corrals. Thomas's eyes danced when he saw Caleb on a tall paint horse that was prancing and tossing its head. The boy looked good up there—he looked like he knew what he was doing. Thomas felt certain Aida would not put the boy on a horse he couldn't handle and was content to watch without comment.

Aida turned when she heard them behind her and saw Harley holding the spray of flowers. She nodded at him and smiled, "Charlie buy those for you?" once again causing Thomas to snort and cover his mouth.

Harley Ponyboy handed over the flowers without smiling and said, "The Professor sent these." He had the feeling Aida didn't like him. *Maybe she still thought he was the one who hit George Custer in the head with the shovel.*

Charlie stepped up and handed Aida the letter that went with the flowers. He tilted his head slightly and smiled. "Dr. Custer was up most of the night writing this. He had a wastebasket full of them before he came up with this one."

Aida didn't change expression, just stuck the letter in the flower arrangement and left for the house.

Thomas and Harley had already settled themselves along the top rail of the fence. Charlie joined them, throwing an occasional glance back over his shoulder at Aida as she made her way stiffly up the path to the house. He saw no sign she was pleased.

"That boy is a chip off the ol' blockhead," Harley declared nudging Thomas Begay, as they watched the way Caleb sat the paint gelding as it trotted around the pen.

"Yep," Charlie said, "it looks like he may have learned a thing or two since he got here."

Thomas studied his son and beamed. The boy was now nearly as good a rider as his sister.

Ida Marie Begay cantered a great circle around the corral and waved at her father as she passed. He gave her a thumbs-up and thought, *Aida Winters has been very good to these children, just as she was to their mother.* Thomas was not one to forget a favor.

When, finally, Charlie went up to the house to tell Aida they were leaving, he found her still sitting on the veranda holding the open letter from George Armstrong Custer.

"Charlie, would you ask George to drop by here on his way back to Albuquerque?" She moved to the edge of the veranda. "I would like to know now what he found in that *kiva* here in the canyon." She looked up the valley in the direction of the ruin. "Hiram Buck's old mother, before she died, would not come anywhere near this ranch. Said something bad happened in that canyon before the Anasazi left. Some said the old woman was a witch. She was mean enough and ugly enough to be a witch, that's for damn sure." She let the letter drop to her side. "Let me get you boys some ice-tea. Seems I've forgotten my manners, what with all this," she said as she waved a hand at the flowers. "You're welcome to stay for supper too, should you be of a mind."

Charlie shook his head. "Aida, we've got to be getting back to town. We have to meet some of the crew at three o'clock and load supplies. As it is, I'm guessing it will be well after dark when we get back to camp."

Aida nodded and folded the letter, then put it in her pocket.

Charlie borrowed her phone to call Sue. His wife had not answered when he had called from town. Again, he did not get an answer, but left messages from Thomas and Harley for their wives, and yet another one for Sue, a more personal one. He hoped Aida, just outside, couldn't hear him. He was a little embarrassed, but that didn't prevent him from saying what he needed to say.

Aida Winters walked with Charlie back to the corrals and called the children in off the horses. She told Thomas how happy she was to have them spend part of their vacation there. "Those two are making 'kids' horses' out of some of these old broomtails That's money in the pocket for me. I'll see they take some of it home for school clothes."

Thomas nodded and again saw his debt to Aida Winters increase.

After they had said their goodbyes and the three Dinè were on their way back to town, Harley Ponyboy, looked in the rearview mirror and admitted, "That's a nice woman, that Aida Winters. I never really been around no white women, other than a few school teachers at boarding school." He smiled. "But I was never really in school enough ta get used to them either."

"Well, one thing's for sure," Charlie, said. "She thinks the world of those kids. And I believe she's having some second thoughts about George Custer, too."

Thomas nodded. "I hope so. It might get a little lonely for her out here after school takes up."

~~~~~~~

It was nearly midnight when the Suburban crawled and bounced its way back up the wash to George Custer's dig. They were all pretty well worn out from the bone-jarring trip and left most of the supplies for the next morning, when more help would be available to ferry it up to the camp.

At daylight, when Charlie yawned himself awake, the professor was standing at the tent flap, holding two steaming cups of coffee. "Good morning," he grinned, and then, "How did things go yesterday?"

Charlie kicked off the blanket, and sat up on the edge of the cot, "Okay, I think, we got everything on the list and I picked up the mail."

"No, I mean with Aida—how did that go?"

"Well, you know Aida." Charlie stretched and yawned some more. "It's hard to get a take on what she's thinking sometimes." Charlie had slept the few hours in his clothes and had only to pull his boots on. As he took the cup of coffee, he didn't look directly at George Custer. "She did say she would like for you to stop back through, when you're finished with the project here." And then he flashed his old mentor a smile. "I guess that's saying *something*." He ran a pocket-comb through his hair. "She mentioned too, she thinks it's time she knew what's in the kiva up at her place."

The professor looked down for a moment "She's probably better off not knowing what's in that kiva. But, maybe she's right. Maybe it is time." The Professor put his cup down on the makeshift desk and sat heavily back in his camp chair. "Her place may never seem quite the same to her, though, once she knows."

"So, I'm guessing you expect to find the same here in this kiva?" Charlie was skeptical and it showed.

"I know exactly what I'm going to find here." The professor sighed and moved some papers about his desk. "Charlie, years ago, do you recall me mentioning a Dr. Averill McCarthy?"

Charlie thought for a moment "He was once a colleague of yours, as I recall."

"An old Professor of mine, actually, first active in the science back when most reports from the field were chiefly supposition and conjecture. There was tree ring dating and later, carbon 14 analysis, of course, but the rest was mostly seat-of-your-pants stuff." Dr. Custer absentmindedly stirred his coffee. "Everyone had their own ideas in those days, but archaeologists were a pretty regimented little fraternity." He peered at Charlie over the rim of his cup. "What I have been doing these past few years is retracing a succession of sites already investigated by Averill McCarthy back at the very start of his career. Even then, he knew what he was onto, but he also knew he didn't have the technology to prove it. The good doctor was old school, deeply imbedded in his particular social strata of academia. I suppose he didn't want to rock the boat."

There was a fly buzzing around the tent, and Professor Custer followed its flight as he reached for the fly swatter. "Dr. McCarthy took me into his confidence in the latter days of our association and made me privy to his research on the 'Migration.' He knew technology was advancing at an astonishing rate and felt one day his theories could be proven." The fly landed on George's desk, and he was ready for it. He was a meticulous man, in most regards, and flies were on his hit list. Brushing what was left of it from a notebook to the trash, he looked up. "Others have since come to the same conclusions, but now we have the means to *prove* what once was only conjecture."

Charlie was fascinated but couldn't help asking, "You're not saying this was a common scenario in the *kivas* you've investigated, are you, George?"

"No, no, not by a long shot! Quite rare, in fact." George became animated, waving an arm in dismissal. "The old man must have worked dozens of ceremonial chambers without finding anything such as this. But, there are three sites in the direct line of migration that do show a similar 'scenario,' as you call it—enough to establish a basis for McCarthy's hypothesis." George Custer grew even more agitated. "I had almost given up hope of finding further corroboration, when I was made aware of Aida's ranch. Now, there was a kiva unknown to McCarthy— incredibly well preserved, too, right down to the coprolites." He raised a finger and thumb and held them apart to emphasize his point. "Those ancient, desiccated droppings will once and for all settle the question of what sometimes happened during the latter stages of the great migration.

The professor's enthusiasm was contagious and caused Charlie to wonder aloud, "How soon do you figure you'll know something here?"

"I expect it will be the end of the week before we are down to base level—at least, for this last occupation, which is what we are most interested in. I have people working on general site evaluation and period integration, but only a select few will participate in this final work in the kiva." He studied Charlie for a moment. "I do not want word of this final phase of the study to get out before I publish my paper. You are welcome to be there, Charlie. In fact, a credible, unaffiliated witness to this last stage of the excavation might come in handy at some point."

"Exciting as all this is, George, I hope you are prepared for the possible repercussions. The Hopi in particular are not going to be happy to see this work published. Their former public support in passing the 'Indian Reparations Act' could evaporate. The Navajo Nation has steadily been forced to relinquish and negotiate land rights in these ongoing legal maneuvers. The Hopi's main argument to the government is their Anasazi connection to ancestral ceremonial places and burials in this area."

Charlie wanted to make himself very clear in this. "Your findings, if proven, could be a major setback in regard to continued public sympathy and support for the Hopi Nation. They are not going to take that laying down."

"Charlie, I believe we have already seen a reaction right here in the attacks on this camp." George Custer lowered his voice and went on, "The Hopi are a good and intelligent people. Only a few highly placed instigators may be involved in this, thus far, but that could easily be fanned into a groundswell of activism among the Pueblo people, should our current antagonist's activities not be curtailed. They are smart and apparently well funded. It's the sort of thing that can get out of hand."

The professor paused and flashed Charlie a grim smile. "As I have said before, my work is a matter of science. How it might affect any particular group is irrelevant in the face of truth."

Charlie sat back down on his cot and stared at the canvas floor. "I did make a phone call in town regarding information on Ira Buck, and another one to the Bureau of Land Management district office to report what's happened out here. I'm supposed to get back to them this afternoon. I'm going to take a ride up to the point of the mesa later and try to get out on the radio. Maybe we can get some idea of how Ira Buck fits in this and possibly who he's tied in with."

Dr. Custer was not so sure. "I doubt we'll find out much more about Ira Buck than we already know. I am more concerned that he might have confederates right here in camp."

"You mean Tanya Griggs?"

"I'm reserving judgment on Tanya, but there is another person that might bear watching.

"Who's that?" This took Charlie by surprise, as he had not considered anyone other than the Hopi girl.

"I've had my eye on Ted Altman—the undergrad student from Oklahoma State. There's something not quite right about him. His resume is a bit sketchy. I took him on mainly due to his medical training—an important consideration on these isolated projects, as we have already seen." The professor paused and then thoughtfully concluded, "He seems awfully friendly with Tanya Griggs, though they are both attractive young people and that's to be expected. And granted, he's new to the science and just now gaining an understanding of our work here, but his interest seems somehow superficial." Here the professor seemed to think of something he had not previously considered. "I suppose there could be a logical explanation for all this, but I can't help feel we're missing something right here under our noses."

Charlie reflected on this for only a moment before saying, "Why don't we let Thomas have a talk with Ted Altman before we get too heavily invested. You know..." He smiled, "Indian to Indian. Thomas is pretty good at figuring out where people are coming from."

"Invested?" George Custer grinned, "You mean in our own paranoia?"

"Something like that, I guess."

"Fine, just have Thomas keep it casual. I wouldn't let on Ted's suspect in any way. You could be right about the paranoia."

The morning worksheet listed both Thomas Begay and Ted Altman assigned to the middens heap off the edge of the ruins. Thomas had already been clearing and gridding the area for nearly a week. They were now ready to do some light trenching on the peripheries to establish some sort of perimeter.

Later, as Charlie and Harley talked with Professor Custer in the open area of camp, they cast the occasional furtive glance at Thomas Begay and Ted Altman hard at work on the middens.

Harley, who had worked with Ted Altman the previous week, was of the opinion their suspicion was unwarranted. "I do not see why you are picking on this guy. He ain't even from around here. He seems very interested in our Navajo culture, too. He says all Indians have to stick together, and the Navajo, being one of the largest tribes, should take a lead in Indian rights and that stuff. I don't see anything wrong with that."

"Really, Harley?" Charlie had been curious about what Harley Ponyboy and Ted Altman talked about, as he had seen them in what appeared to be earnest conversation on several occasions. "What else do you and Ted talk about?"

"Oh, you know, mostly that big Indian movement outa Oklahoma, and how much good they have done for the native peoples." Harley looked up the hill and nodded. "He said the 'movement' was going ta have a booth at the inter-tribal ceremonials at Gallup this year. He told me I should go by and sign up. He thinks I could be a big help recruiting less advantaged people in the remoter parts of the reservation."

Charlie Yazzie exchanged glances with the professor, then pursed his lips and nodded. He allowed that might be a good thing, but wanted to know, "What exactly does Ted himself do in this 'movement' Harley?"

"I don't know *exactly*. Ted said he couldn't say a whole lot about it just yet, but he said it would be a good thing to have a part in."

When lunchtime came, Thomas Begay picked up his sack lunch at the mess tent and found Charlie Yazzie and Harley Ponyboy already eating with the professor in front of his tent. Charlie moved over on the cedar log and made room for Thomas.

"How did things go up at the middens?" the Professor wanted to know.

"Pretty good. We almost have the perimeters staked out and will finish gridding it this afternoon. It's a big trash heap; bigger than I thought."

Charlie grinned. "How did you get along with Ted this morning?"

"Good," Thomas grinned back. "I can get along with a rattlesnake, as long as it rattles now and then," (a statement that would later come back to haunt him).

"Did he sign you up for the Indian movement?"

"No, but he did tell me all about it. He said it would be right up my alley. Not sure what he meant by that."

The professor was grinning now, too, and said, "Hang in there. I'm sending Harley over to help you boys out this afternoon. Keep your ears open."

That night at supper all the Indian crewmembers seemed to gravitate to one end of the table. They had now all worked together and were better acquainted and, the fact is, they were curious about one another. Charlie sat at the very end of the table and Thomas and Harley were at either side. Ted Altman and Tanya Griggs took seats directly across from one another. As the meal progressed, Charlie thought he detected a certain animosity on the part of the Hopi girl when it came to Ted Altman. He wasn't sure when this had come about, as they had seemed on very good terms before the accident, but, when he thought back. *One of the undergrads did say he heard them arguing in the women's tent after the cave in.*

"Could you pass me that salt shaker, Harley?" Ted smiled and took the shaker, saying thanks in return. He seemed self-assured, cocky even, and kept glancing across with a smirk at Tanya Griggs.

The young Hopi sat next to Thomas. Other than a few light scratches and a small cut on her cheek, she appeared to have suffered but little injury in the kiva accident that morning. Thomas spoke to her several times, but she had little to say in return. Even Harley, whom she liked, tried to draw her out a few times but nothing came of it. Bob Mills, the forensic dentist, had taken a seat on the other side of the girl, and she did carry on a bit of conversation with him, though she didn't seem particularly pleased to do so.

Finally, Bob looked over at Harley and asked, "How's that tooth doing, Harley? Does it feel like its taking root?"

"Maybe it's still too soon to tell, doc. It still wiggles a little, but it feels okay. I try ta be careful when I eat."

Bob nodded back and said he thought it might take as much as two or three weeks before it took root. Everyone had heard the story of how Harley had his tooth knocked out and the curious still occasionally asked to see it.

Ted Altman looked down the table at Charlie and said, "Looks like you're the only one to come out of that little scrape with no damage."

Charlie mumbled something about being lucky and concentrated on his food.

Thomas's jaw had gone down considerably since the incident, but he tried to show it to its best advantage in light of the discussion. "Charlie's always been lucky that way. When we played high school ball he always wound up on top of the pile." Everyone else chuckled at this, but Ted Altman didn't.

When all but a few left the supper table and the dishes were cleared away, George Custer moved down the table to sit with the three Dinè. They refilled their coffee cups and relaxed.

The professor spoke first, "There seems to be a bit of animosity in the tribal ranks this evening."

Charlie agreed. "Yep, that pretty much came out of nowhere, too. Tanya and Ted were fine this morning. She seemed grateful for his attention after the cave-in." Charlie took a drink of his coffee. "I was finally able to get out on the truck radio this morning. I had to go almost to the top of the mesa before I was high enough to get a signal—still some static, but I could hear all right." He studied what he was about to say for a moment and then, "I think I may have learned something that could shed some light on Tanya's relationship with Ted Altman"

George Custer looked up from his cup. "And what might that be?"

"Ira Buck is a member of that militant Indian rights movement. His priors show two arrests for 'failure to disperse' in two different rallies here in the Four Corners. Both rallies were sponsored by the movement."

Thomas spoke up, "The Bucks never struck me as the kind to join any political demonstrations."

Charlie held up a hand. "Wait, it gets better. Those rally arrest records show Myra and Steven Griggs as participants as well. They are all members of the militant splinter group known as American Indians for Political Change, or AFPAC, among themselves."

"What about Ted Altman? Was he on the arrest list?" the Professor asked.

"No," Charlie said, "he wasn't on the list, but he is a longtime member of AFPAC. Those rallies were both here in our area, one of them at the dedication of a dam, and the other outside Mesa Verde Park. Altman was not a part of them as far as anyone knows. If Altman is in this, he's a recent addition, possibly called in for just this occasion."

Thomas lifted his head. "What about our little run-in with Ira Buck? Did you get ahold of Ute tribal police?"

"I did." Charlie stirred his coffee without looking at it. "There is now a warrant out for him as well. Apparently, the old sheepherder we met on our way into town later called in and reported him, too. They said this isn't the first time they've tried to apprehend Ira Buck. But this time they've turned it over to the FBI—these incidents all took place on reservations."

The professor stood up. "I think it's about time I had another talk with Tanya Griggs."

Harley, already standing at the tent flap, said, "She's just outside. I heard her talking a minute ago. They are putting together a little campfire out there."

Charlie stood to leave as well, "I don't think it would hurt to have a word with Ted Altman, either. I think the professor might be right about him."

Thomas grinned as he rose from his chair. "You're not letting that Altman guy get to you, are you, college boy?"

Charlie grinned back, "Not yet, I'm not."

When the four men filed outside, they saw Tanya Griggs heading over to her tent, and George Custer followed after her, while the other three joined the group at the fire.

Looking around, Charlie turned to Thomas and said, "I don't see Altman, do you?"

Thomas scanned the crew and said, "He's not here, as far as I can see, but he could have gone to the latrine, or maybe he turned in early."

"Latrine, maybe, but I don't believe he turned in. He's usually one of the last to leave these little get-togethers." Just as Charlie was about to ask Harley to check the latrine, there came a bloodcurdling scream from the women's tent.

When Harley and Thomas reached the tent, Professor Custer was coming out with Tanya Griggs in tow.

"There's a rattlesnake in there! It's on her cot. Better get a shovel." The professor moved past them and held onto Tanya's arm as he helped her back to the fire.

Charlie Yazzie, who was not quite to the tent, heard George Custer's order, turned back, picked up a shovel from beside the mess tent, and returned to the group, which had thinned considerably at the mention of a snake. Charlie pushed his way in past Thomas and was back out in only a minute with the nearly decapitated snake on the end of the shovel.

"Hopi are usually not afraid of snakes," he declared as he passed.

Thomas, who jumped aside with remarkable agility, called after him, "She's only half Hopi, Charlie. It must have been that other half that screamed." Thomas had seen very few rattlesnakes on the reservation and certainly not one like this.

At the fire, Professor Custer pronounced it a "Pink Hopi Rattler," a localized subspecies often associated with the Hopi Snake Dance Ceremony. He had never heard of one this far north, though they were not uncommon on the Hopi Reservation.

A strange calm fell over Tanya Griggs as she sat by the fire surrounded by her fellow team members. "The boys of our village play with snakes from the time they are little and are taught not to be afraid of them." She seemed mesmerized by the rattler, which still gave an occasional twitch as it lay in the firelight. "The priests keep a few snakes year-round to teach the boys, but they only keep each snake a short while. Girls are not a part of this."

Tanya gazed vacantly around the group. Her voice seemed measured and distant. "My people employ all sorts of snakes in the snake dance in August, mostly harmless ones these days. Only a few of these Hopi rattlesnakes are used now, and then only by priests." She again glanced at the snake and a tremor ran through her. "The Hopi believe snakes are messengers from the underworld and try never to harm one." She looked reproachfully at Charlie Yazzie as she said this.

Harley, too, was distressed at the killing of the snake. He also had been taught the snake is a creature to be protected, and he would not knowingly have harmed one. Anthropologists maintain this is a belief passed on to the Navajo from the Hopi themselves, as has been the case with a good many other Navajo beliefs. When the Navajo first came into the country, it was with only a basic hunter-gatherer culture. They perceived the ultra-religious Hopi and their more complicated ceremonies to be powerful medicine and adopted as much of it as they were able to integrate with their own beliefs. Even the traditional stories of Spider Woman and the Hero Twins apparently originated with the Hopi. Some think the Zuni had a hand in some of this, as well.

The professor kneeled down, almost next to Tanya's ear and whispered, "Tanya, you don't think this snake is a chance encounter, do you?" Then he said in a quiet but firm voice, "Charlie said the snake might have been placed on your cot as a warning. What sort of message do you think this snake was bringing you, Tanya?"

Staring vaguely past the professor, the young woman seemed to have trouble forming her words. "The message was not just for me... the message was for all of us." As she said this, she tugged at her sleeve, pulling it back—to expose two purple puncture wounds on her upper arm.

By the time Charlie and Professor Custer had a "soft" tourniquet above the bite marks, Tanya's forehead had already broken out in beads of perspiration, and the arm, a mottled grey-blue, began to swell noticeably. The young woman moaned softly to herself as the professor mobilized his people. At the Suburban, the rear seats were let down and a makeshift bed was quickly arranged in the back.

An improvised litter, carried by a relay of the strongest crewmembers, was loaded, and she was on her way out of the canyon in a matter of minutes. Dental student Bob Mills had taken charge of the evacuation and rode with Tanya in the back of the vehicle.

Charlie and Thomas jumped in Charlie's truck and made for the point of the mesa. Charlie hoped he could radio the rescue unit in Cortez to intercept the Suburban—a vial of anti-venom delivered en route might save precious time. Professor Custer thought it useless to try for any of the smaller towns; the probability of them having the serum would be chancy at best.

At camp, Harley Ponyboy and George Custer were looking for Ted Altman, but Altman was nowhere to be found.

About midnight Charlie and Thomas returned with the news that a helicopter from Cortez had met the Suburban at the highway and airlifted Tanya Griggs back to a waiting hospital team in Cortez.

"The doctor is guarded in his assessment of Tanya's chances." Charlie Yazzie's voice was strained as he made the announcement to the anxious group. "He told me a bite on the ankle or lower leg is one thing, but the upper arm is much more complicated and dangerous."

At daylight the following morning, the sound of sheep bells roused Thomas from a light and troubled sleep. As he pulled on his clothes, he nudged Harley awake in the next bunk and said softly, "I think we got company."

The tiny tinkle of sheep bells is a shepherd's early warning system and discloses not only the location, but also the temperament of the flock. Thomas, like most rural Navajo growing up, was well versed in the language of the bells.

George Custer, the camp's earliest riser, had already left his tent and was putting together a pot of coffee in the mess tent. Charlie was up as well and washing at the tin basin outside when he heard the bells.

Thomas and Charlie arrived at the edge of the clearing just as the flock broke over the ridge. It was the old man they met on their recent trip to town, and when he saw the two of them approaching he waved and caused his horse to wade towards them through the sheep. With a movement of his arm and a whistle, he directed the dogs to hold the flock at the edge of the clearing.

Thomas raised a hand and called above the noise of the sheep, "Ho, Grandfather, you must have camped nearby to get here before the sun."

When the old man pulled his horse up in front of them, they could see it was lathered in sweat. "No, Grandson, I pushed these sheep most of the night to get out of 'Splits In Two.' It is too crowded down there in the big canyon. I thought I had best come back up here on top. The feed's not so good here, but the company is better, I think."

"Crowded?" Thomas gave the old man a quizzical smile, "How so, Grandfather?"

The old man considered carefully before answering. "There are strange things going on in the canyon these last few nights. I have seen people down there who have no business in this country." The old man paused as he regarded Thomas Begay. "I am not so old and scary as to be easily frightened in my own country, but these people's coming and going were not natural and made me nervous." The old man's Navajo was spoken quickly and barely above a whisper. Charlie was having a hard time understanding all he said.

"Did you see the big man with the bad hand down there Grandfather?" Thomas was anxious to hear if he had again seen the Ute who had wreaked such havoc on them."

"No, Grandson, I am glad to say I did not see that one. Maybe he died of his wound, or maybe he is off doing evil someplace else." The old man pursed his lips. "But I did see a woman who spoke Hopi, and her man, who was white and yet understood what she was saying all right." The old man slid stiffly off his horse, and they could hear his joints creak as he straightened and slowly moved his head from side to side to ease his neck.

Thomas introduced Charlie, who for the first time learned the old man's name. It was Hastiin Bahzhoni—loosely translated it meant, "Mr. Pleasant One. It seemed a curious name, even for a Dinè and certainly not as common as some others. There is no accounting for Navajo names or how they come about. In the old days they were subject to change arbitrarily, sometimes due to a life circumstance, or more often, just on a whim. In the case of Hastiin Bahzohni the name seemed appropriate. He had grown up and lived most of his life within fifty miles of where he now stood and was well thought of.

"Last night in the canyon," he said, carefully picking his words, "I watched those people from a high place in the rocks and in the fullness of the moon and light of their fire, saw more than I wanted to see."

"What were they doing, Grandfather?" Thomas Begay felt a shiver go up his back, even as the sun's first warm rays touched him. It was a dangerous business to spy on shape-shifters and witches in the dead of night. *It is said the Yeenaaldiooshii never sleep.*

"The woman was praying, Grandson, and singing. She made snake signs on the ground and called to beings from the underworld. We Navajo and Hopi share many things, but calling on the dead and their *chindi* is only for witches."

Thomas Begay did not like hearing this kind of talk and asked, "Were there only the two people down there, Grandfather?" He was careful not to say the old man's name—not to his face—especially when there was talk of witches that might have the power to listen in."

"It is funny you should ask that, it must have been about midnight when another person appeared—an Indian as far as I could tell, but not like you and me. Maybe he had been asleep and I had not noticed him before. I could see he was not from around here. He talked English but not like you. He sounded more like those 'bureau' people that come poking around asking questions sometimes."

The old man seemed to ponder for a moment. "Those Hopi must have gone for him at some point as there is no way he could have come into the canyon at night by himself. Or maybe they just conjured him up out of nothing. I have lived all my life in this country and from time to time, I still get turned around in 'Splits In Two.' There is no way he could have found his way there by himself. I don't know why those people would be running back and forth, up and down the canyon in the night, unless they are Yeenaaldiooshii, or some other witches who do their work in the dark." The old man concluded by saying, "Anyway, you said I should tell you of anything out of the ordinary, so here I am saying these things to you." The old man shook himself free of the bad thoughts, "Do you have coffee, Grandson? My bones have taken a chill this morning."

Thomas smiled, "Yes, Grandfather, there is coffee and more." Then, ever the herder himself, he asked, "Are your sheep all right where they are?"

The old man watched his flock for a moment. "Yes, they are tired and hungry from that little trip up the canyon, but there is enough feed here to keep them occupied. The dogs should hold them awhile with no trouble."

The old man tied his horse and followed along to the mess tent. George Custer saw them coming and had a speckled-blue coffee pot at the end of the table along with cups and all the fixings. The mess crew of the day was already at work on a huge breakfast, and the old man licked his lips at the smell of frying bacon.

Harley Ponyboy came in and reported there still was no sign of Ted Altman. His cot had not been slept in and it appeared some of his things were missing as well. Harley did, however, find *something* in Ted Altman's tent, a small, covered wicker basket lying empty under his bunk. Harley put the basket on the table, and the Professor picked it up and examined it as only a scientist can.

"This is a very old ceremonial basket; the kind the Hopi keep their snakes in." He held the open basket to his nose and sniffed, then wrinkled his nose, nodded, and passed it to Charlie. "You can still smell the musk in it."

Thomas said, "Well, that pretty much explains where the snake came from, I guess, but why would Ted Altman want to put a rattlesnake in Tanya's bed?"

Dr. Custer spoke again, "Tanya said that snake was a warning meant for all of us. This wouldn't be the first time a Hopi priest has sent a snake as a warning. They may not have meant for it to bite her, maybe only rattle a warning, something Tanya would have been well acquainted with." The professor paused. "Not many know it, but Hopi priests who handle the rattlesnakes 'milk' them of their venom just before they are used in the ceremonies. This limits the effects of a bite should one happen. It takes a few days for the snake to replenish the venom, and they are usually quite tranquil in the interim. They seem to know intuitively that their major defense has been compromised." The professor turned grim, "Rattlesnakes don't always rattle, though, and also, Ted Altman may have had a different agenda."

Charlie, who had remained quiet, now weighed in, "If that is the case, someone may have misjudged the time factor. It's hard to believe Tanya's parents would have a hand in something they thought might harm their own daughter, if indeed that *is* them down in the canyon. If they are involved with Ted Altman in this 'militant group,' it could be a warning of even worse things to come. It's obvious they don't give up easily."

The old sheepherder, Hastiin Bahzhoni, had listened closely to all this talk of snakes and Hopi witches and, understanding more English than he let on, hurriedly finished his breakfast and was anxious to be on his way. He took his leave, saying he would keep his sheep up on the mesa for the time being and would keep an eye out for strangers.

Midmorning, a BLM officer came by and reported Tanya's condition was improved. She was lucid and alert though certainly not yet out of the woods. There was still some concern she might eventually lose her left arm. This threw a pall over the camp, and it was Dr. George Custer who seemed most affected. The Professor felt he was somehow to blame and berated himself over the incident. "I should have known someone other than myself would eventually get hurt." He sighed, "I should have seen this coming."

The BLM officer, who was the district supervisor, also mentioned that Ira Buck was still at large, even though an APB had been issued by local law enforcement. It was thought the fugitive might be hiding out in the backcountry or possibly had sought refuge with his northern clansmen. Both Ute and Navajo tribal police had been notified. Ira Buck had apparently not found treatment for his shattered hand at any local facility. Several of the more prominent native healers had been contacted, as well, but denied knowledge of any such injury.

Before leaving, the officer drew the professor aside and said he had brought him a sealed letter from Tanya, passed along by Bob Mills, who had stayed with the girl throughout her ordeal. He looked the professor directly in the eye as he passed him the envelope. "I hope, if this letter contains anything pertinent to the investigation, you would immediately relay that information to the proper authorities."

Custer nodded and assured him he would. The Professor had given Bob Mills leave to stay with the stricken girl as long as he thought necessary. He thought Bob was smitten with her and had her best interest at heart. He had never thought the same about Ted Altman. In any case, he felt it best she not be left alone until everything was sorted out.

Dr. Custer had previously posted rotating guards at the dig, but now thought better of it and announced to the team, "It's not worth putting any more of the crew in harm's way, especially now that we're already short three workers. These people are even more dangerous than we first thought. We'll stay on the alert. Charlie and Thomas have volunteered, along with Harley and myself, to take turns patrolling the dig at night. We will work in pairs and alternate four-hour shifts. I'm convinced these people will be back. It's only a question of when." The professor hesitated and then added, "Charlie has a revolver and Harley has that shotgun patched back together, so at least we will be armed should it come to that." This last statement caused a ripple of consternation to pass through the crew. Later, several of them privately voiced the opinion that perhaps the entire project should be shelved until such time it could be deemed safe to continue.

The professor motioned for Charlie Yazzie to follow him to his tent, as Thomas and Harley trailed the rest of the crew up to the dig and the day's work. At his desk, George Custer opened the multi-page letter and silently began to read. Only occasionally did he glance up at Charlie. When he finished, he passed him the letter without comment.

Charlie took his time, reading some portions of the letter twice. When he was through, he carefully folded the pages and returned them to George Custer. "How much longer do you think it will take to finish the kiva excavation?"

"Five, maybe six days, and an equal amount of time to photograph, catalogue, and make a field evaluation of any materials recovered. I've already assigned more workers to speed up the process; something I really didn't want to do. Much of the information and verification we're looking for may take weeks, if not months, of forensic investigation back at the lab. But I will know what I need to know right here, and soon."

George toyed with the folded letter before putting it in the cardboard file-cabinet beside his desk. The two men sat staring quietly at one another, each thinking their own thoughts. The professor spoke first, with the opinion they were too close now to quit and leave the site to who knew what sort of vandalism or damage. "One way or the other, this is our last shot at this particular piece of the puzzle. It would be a travesty to leave this final page unturned."

Charlie agreed. When he left the Professor's tent, he again went over the letter in his mind. The letter had noted Bob had not left Tanya's side—sleeping in a chair and taking his meals in the hospital cafeteria. *If what Tanya maintained was true, it might be a very good thing he was there.*

She said she only applied for the Custer expedition after a long and drawn-out confrontation with her mother. Her father had taken her mother's side, as he often felt compelled to do. She, however, could not bring herself to support her parent's dogged position regarding the damage that could be done the Hopi nation. Damage, they felt, would most assuredly come with the publication of Dr. George Custer's work and upcoming paper.

She had been raised in a family of academic professionals dedicated to scientific discovery and truth. That her parents would forsake the very beliefs they had instilled in her was beyond all reasoning. She intended to do her own due diligence and see for herself what was at stake, and no amount of argument would change her mind.

Tanya first thought Ted Altman had a genuine interest in her and had no idea he might have been sent by her parents to monitor both the dig, and her. She thought it only a coincidence that Ted was a member of the same politically active movement as her parents. Many Indian intellectuals of her acquaintance were members of one group or another—mostly just to make a social statement, in her opinion. Tanya said her first inkling that things with Ted Altman might not be as they seemed came after the cave-in at the kiva. She had gone up the hill earlier than usual that morning, even before George Custer. While she was not authorized to work the kiva that day, she was excited they were getting so close to their goal. Tanya thought it couldn't hurt to slip into the kiva for just a quick look. As she knelt to examine a patch of freshly turned earth, oddly out of place, she heard a noise and caught just a glimpse of someone on the kiva rim. That was the last thing she remembered until she regained consciousness in her tent with the medic, Ted Altman, in attendance.

Later, she said, it would stick in her mind that the person on the rim of the kiva that morning appeared to be wearing a khaki shirt. A shirt like Ted Altman wore nearly every day—not an unusual item of apparel among the crew—and certainly not indicative of wrongdoing, yet the thought lingered. When Tanya was feeling better, the two had talked quietly there in her tent, and Ted remained solicitous and concerned.

She also mentioned that several people had dropped by on their lunch hour, but Altman told them she could not be disturbed. As the afternoon wore on, Ted's mood had slowly changed, and he quietly began badgering her about the Indian movement and how important it was that they should all stick together. He made it clear where he stood and finally went so far as to admit he had been in touch with her parents, and that they were very upset with her—to the point, he warned, that something might have to be done about it. Tanya said she then became angry and they quarreled.

The letter was detailed and concise in assessment of conversations with Ted Altman and reading between the lines allowed Charlie to think she might be above suspicion in any wrongdoing.

Charlie couldn't help but wonder how Ted Altman had been in such close contact with the interlopers without being discovered and thought, *The professor had never trusted Altman from the start and kept a close eye on his coming and going. In a tight knit group like this, it would be hard to get away with very much. Could there be yet another person in their crew involved?*

In the following days Charlie was amazed at how much work was accomplished. In Dr. Custer's opinion they were well ahead of schedule despite being short handed. Everyone was working from near daylight to dark and the pace was beginning to tell as tempers began to fray. The professor and the three Dinè were not only pulling night guard-duty but also putting in a good number of hours on the excavation itself. Charlie was almost surprised there was no further interference or sign of their antagonists. He suspected, however, that the closer they got to their goal, the more likely another incident became.

On the third night, Professor Custer and Harley Ponyboy were on their second rotation of duty and were having a hard time keeping their eyes open. They were lying almost prone on a high ledge above the site. The ledge had long been home to several beehive-like masonry storage facilities shored up by a low rock retaining wall. The Professor had selected the location himself, and while the path leading to it was difficult, Harley agreed it would allow them to cover the usual approaches to the dig without exposing their position.

Thomas and Charlie had finished their last shift of the night and had retired to their beds when the explosion came, and like everyone else they were left wide awake and deafened by the blast.

The explosion overwhelmed the camp with reverberating shockwaves filled with debris. The sturdy expedition tents were pelted with small bits of wood and masonry—several came down completely, trapping their unfortunate occupants in a welter of canvas in the process.

Charlie came instantly awake, unable to hear, yet unsure of the reason. The professor's tent, some distance from the others and protected by the piñon grove, suffered the least damage. The stovepipe collapsed, as did the rear support poles. The ridgepole, down at the back, left it more of a teepee than a wall tent. Charlie's first thought was of Harley and the professor on their ledge above the alcove. *Surely they couldn't have survived such an explosion almost directly below them.*

Charlie and Thomas had come off duty only shortly before and, with breakfast only an hour or so away, neither had bothered to undress, but rather just lay down on their cots with their clothes on. Thomas had not even bothered to remove his boots and was the first one outside the mess tent. A heavy pall of dust hung over the camp, increasing the darkness, and bringing visibility to near zero. Oddly, there were no screams or cries for help. The shock of the blast had rendered everyone temporarily deaf and nearly mute as well. Even in the aftermath, there were few calls for assistance; most extricated themselves and quietly gravitated toward the center of the compound.

Charlie found Thomas immediately and was happy to see him in one piece. He opened his mouth but had either lost the ability to speak... or Thomas remained deaf from the blast and could not decipher what he was saying.

Only two people had to be helped from the rubble of their tents. There were the cuts and contusions one might expect, but miraculously everyone was present and accounted for and with no serious injuries evident. The blast had apparently angled more toward the back of the alcove leaving the bulk of the camp clear of major damage. Only the fate of Harley Ponyboy and the professor remained in question. Thomas and Charlie stood staring silently toward the flattened remains of the ancient village. Charlie couldn't help but think, *What a thousand seasons of the rawest elements had failed to accomplish has been wrought by man in only a few seconds.*

As though moved by a communal will, all but a few stumbled up the slope to the dig. Charlie and Thomas, in the forefront were first to see the stunning effect of the blast. An entire layer of the alcove's ceiling had sheared away, nearly in a single slab, and now covered the major portion of the excavation. The kiva, where the explosion had obviously detonated, was obliterated, the remains now sealed forever in a sandstone tomb. The dust, still heavy in the air, made it nearly impossible to see the ledge where just hours before the professor and Harley had taken up their vigil.

A thin grey line of dawn outlined the mesas to the east, and Charlie estimated it would be another hour before any real assessment of damage could be made.

Several people had the presence of mind to bring along their flashlights and now, in the dust-filtered shafts of light, searched the back wall of the alcove for signs of Harley and the professor. The continued patter of fine debris made all but the most cursory inspection impossible.

As the group huddled, somewhat in doubt, there came a shaky and weak cry from the upper reaches of the alcove.

In the dim light of the flashlights, Charlie glanced at Thomas Begay who seemed not to hear the distant plea.

"You didn't hear that?" Charlie asked, moving closer to Thomas's ear and raising his voice.

"Hear what?" Thomas asked.

"I think it was Harley yelling up on the ledge."

Instantly both men began to climb the slanted slab of sandstone that now buried the dig. Charlie called over his shoulder for someone to bring the ladder from the petroglyph panel at the edge of the alcove. Visibility was slightly better higher up and, in the dim glow of the flashlights, Charlie could make out the ledge and its retaining wall.

The muffled voice came again, but stronger this time and Charlie was now certain it was Harley Ponyboy. "It's Harley all right!" he shouted into Thomas's ear.

Thomas looked up to see a hand waving above the masonry wall. Harley's head became visible as he pulled himself to a kneeling position and looked groggily over the wall at his friends. He had a cut over one eye that was bleeding a steady stream. "Up here!" he cried. "We're okay I think, but the professor has some stuff on top of him." He looked behind him, "I'm gonna need some help!"

Charlie turned to the people below and shouted, "Get some rope up here, and hurry it up with that ladder; the Professor may be hurt."

Thomas was first up the ladder and was taken aback at the sight of Dr. Custer almost totally covered in debris. A log of considerable size had been thrown up and over the retaining wall, and now lay partially across the professor's upper body. Harley Ponyboy was trying to lift the end of what had once been a roof beam of the *kiva*. Harley was strong for one of his stature but still could barely budge the free end of the beam. Even as Thomas arrived and put his back into it, the beam would not move enough to release George Custer. Only when Charlie hurried over from the ladder and added to the effort did the beam grudgingly yield. Luckily for Dr. Custer, the log had been partially supported by the retaining wall and had not brought its full weight to bear.

The professor was coherent through the process and was finally able to raise himself to a sitting position and take stock of his condition. Though he did not look well to Charlie, George Custer declared himself in good enough order, and insisted he was probably no worse off than many others. He was, he said, able to navigate the ladder. Charlie, not so sure, took the precaution of tying a safety line under the professor's arms and, despite his misgivings, they were soon safely back on the ground.

Assessing the destruction in the early light of dawn, there was but one conclusion to be reached—the project would have to be abandoned. It was useless to carry on. Even if the thick slab of sandstone could be removed—an impossibility in itself—there remained the fact that what lay under it would now be of little scientific value. The interlopers had won.

The arduous task of breaking camp was begun and a vehicle readied to evacuate those needing more immediate medical attention. Altogether, there were now only ten members of the expedition left in camp. It was finally decided two of the injured could not wait and were to be sent ahead in advance of the others, along with news of the explosion for authorities. Two uninjured members of the group, one, a young undergrad student who had already been in and out of the dig twice and knew the way, would drive. The young man stoutly protested he would rather stay and help but, at the urging of the professor, finally agreed to go. The other person was Neva Travis, the anthropologist from Western New Mexico University, and while the young driver had been reluctant to go, Neva seemed almost anxious to leave. Charlie had the fleeting thought there might be more to her determination than "looking after the injured." Perhaps fear had shaken her judgment."

The Colombian woman, who was busy packing, would be the only female left in camp. And when she heard Neva had already gone, she, too, thought it odd the anthropologist should be so anxious to leave. She had supposed them to be rather close and felt somewhat at a loss, abandoned even and thought, *The remains of the camp should be packed up in a matter of hours, probably by early afternoon, surely she could have waited.* She didn't understand the need for Neva to leave early and certainly not without saying goodbye.

In the afternoon, when the last loads of equipment were being ferried to the remaining vehicles, Charlie and the professor stood gazing at the remains of the thousand-year-old-settlement. The professor, clearly depressed, still was not ready to abandon the undertaking. "You know," he mused, "we do have one last resort."

"I know." Charlie sighed. "I hesitated to bring it up, given the history between you and Aida." He faltered and then added, "There's something else, something you may not have considered."

The professor gave him a confused look, "What?"

"Don't you think the people who did this will figure your next move will be Aida's ranch?" And here he indicated the destruction in front of them, "Obviously, Myra Griggs, if that's really who is behind all this, is well aware of that kiva and its contents."

George Custer paled and, with a shaking hand covered his eyes for a moment and looked at the ground. "You're right, of course. I must have taken a harder blow to the head than I thought. How could I be so stupid not to factor that in? I've been letting my own selfish ends overrule any semblance of reason. They could be on their way there even as we speak."

"George, what those people have done here today is a serious federal crime. The FBI is already involved and may well be on their trail by now. I'll get in touch with the agent in charge, as soon as we are in radio range. I'm certain our people who went out this morning are already ahead of us on this. They've probably already informed the authorities of what's gone on here. There's nothing else we can do right now. We'll give Aida Winters a heads up on the way into town."

"Yes, yes, you're right. I gave Neva Travis explicit instructions regarding who to notify as soon as they reached town." George Custer thought he had done at least this one thing right.

Charlie hesitated but said nothing. He had not discussed his reservations about Neva Travis with anyone and thought, *Now is not the time to add to Dr. Custer's worries. Clearly, the man is on the brink, and I might still be wrong about Neva Travis.*

George Custer rode with Thomas Begay and Charlie, who drove his own truck, and led the way out.

The Colombian woman and the last of the graduate students were passengers in the follow-up vehicle, which was loaded with more gear and driven by Harley Ponyboy. When assigned the task by Professor Custer, Harley neglected to mention his lack of a driver's license. He had already driven the professor's Suburban into town once— and that while drunk—he thought it reasonable to assume he could do as well sober. Harley had no confidence in drivers not schooled in the rigors of reservation driving. The graduate student was from the city and not of a proper temperament, in his opinion. The Colombian woman did not drive at all.

Thomas knew Harley didn't have a license but kept silent. He, too, thought Harley the best candidate.

The little convoy had gone no more than two miles when Charlie spotted Hastiin Bahzhoni headed their way across a small sage flat. He was traveling quite fast for an old man on an old horse and was stirring up quite a cloud of dust in the process. Charlie gauged their point of convergence, slowed his truck, and came to a standstill just as the old man pulled his horse to a sliding stop. Thomas

Begay was impressed and hoped he could still ride as well, should he reach that age.

Thomas rolled down his window and greeted the old man with a questioning tilt of his chin. He could see Hastiin Bahzohni was in a hurry to tell them something and skipped the niceties.

"Grandson," the old man said in Navajo, trying to catch his breath, "in the middle of the night I got up to check the sheep—something had gotten into them. A coyote maybe. While I was still up and taking a pee, I happened to look down here to the road and saw headlights heading back into your camp." The old man had recovered his wind, slowed down, and now took his time—as older Navajo will eventually do when telling even the most desperate story. "I didn't think too much about it at the time. I supposed it to be one of your people coming back late from a trip to town.

"I had no more than settled the sheep and gone back to sleep when a great thunder shook me out of my blankets. I first thought one of those airplanes that cross in the night had fallen down near your camp. That was the direction the noise came from." The old man took another deep breath. "Again, my silly sheep scattered, and this time it took the dogs some time to gather them. That speckled dog is not as young as he once was and sometimes gives out, leaving the other to do both their jobs. I could not sleep after that and, not long after, I saw the lights coming back this way, and it occurred to me those lights were too close together to be a pickup, probably more like a jeep or some other off-road vehicle."

Thomas interrupted the old man, though he would not ordinarily have done such a thing. "Acheii, I do not mean to be rude, but it is important we know who was at our camp this morning. Our camp is gone now, and we wonder why, and who might have done such a thing."

150

"I was afraid of that." The old man shook his head and looked for a moment in the direction of the ruins. "But it was not those people in the jeep that did it."

Thomas snorted in surprise and stared at the old man. "Why do you say that, Grandfather?"

"Those people did not have time to even get to your camp and return by time I saw them coming back out again." He frowned. "Maybe they became frightened when they heard that big noise and turned back, but they did not have time to reach your camp and return in the amount of time that passed."

Thomas knew the old man had spent his life in this country and knew exactly how much time would be required. He repeated in English for Professor Custer what Hastiin Bahzhoni had said.

Dr. Custer studied on this. "If that is so, it could mean someone in our own group engineered that blast, which could explain why Harley and I didn't spot anyone coming in from the outside. The bugger slid in from inside our own camp."

Charlie Yazzie nodded thoughtfully and was also now convinced their antagonists had yet another confederate among the crew. *How many could there be?*

10

The Reprisal

In Cortez, the professor directed that the graduate student and the Colombian woman were to be reunited with their fellow crewmembers at the motel. The group was further instructed to take the two university vans and return to Albuquerque the following day. He did not mention that he, Charlie, and both Thomas and Harley would continue on to Aida's ranch in a continuation of the original investigation.

At the motel, the undergrad student who had driven the earlier van reported that he had delivered the injured people to the hospital for treatment and was awaiting a report as to their condition and release status. "Neva Travis had me drop her off at the bus station. Said she had 'pressing business' to attend." He said this last part somewhat doubtfully, as though he was not entirely convinced. "She did say she would be in touch, however, and to give everyone her best."

Dr. Custer looked up sharply at this. "Did she mention notifying the authorities, as I asked?"

"Not that I recall, though I guess she could have done that after we dropped her off at the bus station."

Charlie darted a quick glance at the professor and went directly to the office phone.

Professor Custer questioned the student further, "Did you check with Bob Mills about Tanya Griggs while at the hospital?"

"Yes, I did. Bob said she was doing as well as could be expected. I told him I was sure you would be up to check on them."

"That's our first stop after leaving here," the professor confirmed, looking past the young man at Charlie, who was still on the phone. After arranging double accommodations for everyone, (except the Colombian woman, who was given a room to herself), the professor went to stand by Charlie, still engaged on the phone.

Thomas and Harley came in with the group's personal luggage, and most were then off to hot showers. They'd had makeshift showers back in camp, but water was scarce and most had been anticipating the real thing.

Charlie nervously played with the phone's spiral cord as he waited for the FBI agent in charge to come online. He lowered the receiver momentarily to look at the professor. "Neva contacted no one that I've talked to so far. The FBI agent is checking now, but doesn't think he has had anything reported, either. He'll get right back to us to."

The Professor shook his head and thought unkind thoughts about Neva Travis.

By the time the FBI did finally return his call, Charlie and the professor were in their room. Charlie listened intently for several minutes before he thanked the agent and turned to George Custer. "Her bus already arrived in Farmington, and she may have made the afternoon flight out to the Albuquerque hub. They have an agent on the way there to verify."

Custer sighed heavily and, taking the phone, called the hospital to talk to Tanya Grigg's doctor, and hopefully speak to Bob Mills as well. Her doctor, when he finally came on the phone, was encouraging, saying Tanya may not have had the heavy dose of venom her admitting physician first thought. "Tanya told us the Hopi priests sometimes 'milk' the snakes of their venom before handling. This may well have been the case in this instance. For whatever reason, she is recovering beyond our expectations and is almost certain not to require any form of amputation as first reported. The young doctor who was on call and did the original workup is new here. That was his first snake bite case—he learned a lot."

"When can she be released?" Custer was relieved but still anxious for a resolution to the girl's ordeal.

"Two days, maybe. I think that's a reasonable projection." The doctor seemed confident, and this in turn allowed the professor to regain a measure of his own self-confidence. Tanya's doctor said the other two members of the crew would be released the next morning and be able to return to Albuquerque with the rest of their disbanded team. The doctor went on to say that visiting hours were over for the evening, but they could drop by in the morning. "The hospital is quite strict about visiting hours," he said.

After leaving a message for Bob Mills, in which he advised him to take a break and come to the motel for a good night's sleep, Custer hung up the phone in a much improved frame of mind. "She's going to be all right."

Charlie, too, was relieved but thought to himself, *It's not over for Tanya, and I'm not sure she's "all right" as long as the perpetrators are still out there. She could still be in danger.*

The professor, buoyed by the new information, chatted on, "I'm sure we'll see Bob shortly. He definitely needs the break."

"George, do you really think it's okay to leave Tanya alone in the hospital with 'those people' still unaccounted for?"

"Oh, I think so. The other two crew members' room is right next to hers, according to the doctor, and they've promised to keep an eye on her."

Charlie still had his doubts but gave way to the professor's ebullience of spirit, and mentioned it would be nice to have one last get-together with the crew.

"My thoughts exactly. A nice breakfast in the morning would be just the thing. It'll give me a chance to thank everyone for their loyalty and hard work—those that are left, anyway." Here he grimaced, realizing the incongruity of the remark. "In the morning I'll give Aida Winters a call, too. We're long overdue for a chat." Again, Charlie was doubtful. Dr. George Custer's behavior was perplexing. *He is suddenly back to his old state of enthusiasm, and with a newfound confidence. It is no wonder his colleagues find him so disconcerting. This must be what great men were made of then—'the indomitable courage of their convictions.'*

Early the next morning, Charlie, Thomas, and Harley gravitated to the motel's breakfast nook for first coffee.

The professor, still in a rare good humor, soon joined them, "Spoke to Aida this morning, and she has agreed to let the four of us bring a small camp into the canyon for further evaluation of the kiva. I explained what went on at our previous dig and who we think is involved." Here he paused, to look directly at Thomas. "There is no doubt in my mind that Aida's relationship with you and your children played a part in her decision, even though I would like to think there was more to it than that."

The professor smiled and went on. "We'll go into the canyon with a tent and enough gear and food for a week. I have told her we should be in and out in five or six days. There's no excavation required to speak of, and I have all my notes from the last survey to expedite the procedure. We'll not concern ourselves with other than the kiva and, even then, only the information pertinent to our primary investigation."

Charlie hesitated, then brought his thoughts to the table. "What about security?" He studied his three companions "The FBI should have something on the people we've reported very soon. I can't help but believe they will have at least some of them in custody shortly. As I've mentioned, all authorities are giving high priority to this case, and several agencies are working on it as we speak."

The professor looked Charlie directly in the eye. "So I assume the question is... do we wait for the perpetrators to be apprehended or go in now with no assurances of our own safety, or that of the site?" Here the professor raised a questioning eyebrow for the others' input. Everyone had a personal stake in the security issue. "Aida mentioned we could camp there in her barn and make use of her facilities, but I couldn't see leaving the kiva unprotected. And while our security measures didn't help much at the last site, this time there'll be fewer things to worry about; this time we won't have to worry so much about our own people being complicit."

Harley had said nothing during the exchange, but now chimed in, "I think, maybe, Thomas should stay there at the ranch with the kids, at least until we know a little more about where those sorry-ass people have gotten off to."

Charlie agreed. "Aida and the kids need someone around until these people are out of the picture."

The professor held up a finger. "I've thought of that. Tanya Griggs gets out of the hospital tomorrow morning, and Aida says she and Bob can stay there at her place a few days, at least until Tanya's feeling well enough to travel. That way Bob would be right there in the house. Bob's ex-military and can handle himself. He and Thomas both could stay there, and Charlie, myself, and Harley can take care of things up at the dig." And then he said, almost as an afterthought, "Aida has a cabinet full of hunting rifles that belonged to her husband. She says we can borrow what we want, should we feel the need for that sort of thing. We can drop my vehicle off at the hospital this morning, and Bob and Tanya can follow tomorrow morning."

~~~~~~~

When the four men arrived at Aida's ranch, they found Aida in the front yard pruning her rose bushes while the children still slept.

She met them at the gate and told the three Navajo there was coffee in the kitchen and that she had made pies the night before—they were welcome to try them.

Thomas grinned at Harley. "Let's try some of that pie, chubby." He gave Harley a little dig in the ribs. "Charlie don't like pie, do you Charlie?"

Charlie smiled and marshaled the two up the steps and into the house, calling back to Aida, "I'll try to see they don't eat them all."

Professor Custer stayed behind with Aida. "I don't suppose you'd care to come up to the dig with us at some point would you, Aida?" He coughed discreetly. "I thought you might want to be there when we opened up the kiva."

Aida, who had resumed her pruning, turned with a quizzical expression and, disregarding his question, asked, "What were those flowers all about, George?"

"Well Aida, they were just a little token of appreciation. You needn't read in to them any more than that, if the thought offends you."

"What more could I read into them, George?" She turned her full attention to him. "George, you're a womanizer and a drunk. What more am I to make of that?"

The professor drew himself to his full height and looked her calmly in the eye. "Yes, Aida, I am all of that, and more. But I have better expectations." His gaze did not waver, "I have not had a drink in a while, now, and have thought of only one woman since I was last here. I am determined to be a better person in the future."

Aida cocked her head at George Custer. "I wish I could believe that, George, if only for your own sake." She turned back to the roses. "We shall see, George. We shall see."

Thinking this was as good as it was going to get for the present, the professor nodded pleasantly, and followed his companions to the house—he was fond of pie himself.

~~~~~~~

By afternoon, Charlie and Dr. Custer, aided by Harley, had set up a snug little camp near the trickle of water wending its way down the canyon floor. The dirt track Aida's great grandfather had scratched out with team and wagon ran right alongside the stream. Tall ponderosa pines sheltered the front of the cave-like alcove that had been home to so many for so long. It was as near an idyllic setting for an Anasazi settlement as could be imagined. It faced mostly east and was so situated as to catch the first rays of the sun in winter, yet was shaded in the heat of a summer afternoon.

The alcove, carved over eons by ancient winds and water, was neither unusually deep nor overly shallow, but suited the masonry dwellings exactly, without crowding. Nor did the declivity allow for more than two stories, except in the exact arch of the center, where a round tower rose like the turret of a medieval castle, which it would have been well suited for in another time and place. It might have been named Cliff Palace, if that name had not already been taken.

There is an old Ute legend that tells of a party of hunters chancing upon their first such village. They returned to their band with a story of "little people" who ran into holes in the rock cliff at their approach.

The early Ute, before the horse, were a poor people, and there were never enough of them to pose much of a threat to the more numerous Anasazi in their easily defended villages. In time, in fact, they developed a nearly symbiotic relationship with the Pueblo. The Ute, accomplished and far-ranging big game hunters, commonly traded meat and hides for corn and other produce. Like their Paleo-Indian ancestors, the Ute may have snatched the occasional stray woman or child, yet never seemed to assimilate much of the their culture. Farming just wasn't in the Ute genes (as the U.S. government was to discover some thousand years later).

One could see from the exposed streambed that water had once run much stronger in the canyon, with high water probably lasting well into the season. There were little sage plots on either side of the watercourse, and a good bit of corn, beans and squash would have been grown there. This was further evidenced by the remnants of low stone retention walls to collect and channel water, and irrigation ditches to further distribute the life giving flow.

On the mesa top, above the ruins, were large meadow-like flats. In a good snow year the drifts piled wide and deep on the surrounding ridges and provided ground water enough for fine crops the following spring—not every year mind you, but often enough to fill the granaries every few seasons.

At first thought, some might surmise these were a peaceful and quiet little people, simple agrarian farmers. But they would be wrong.

~~~~~~~~

George Custer had warned Aida that she might only want to *hear* about what was in the kiva, rather than actually *see* it; that might prove an entirely different experience.

Aida, for her part, decided otherwise. She wanted to know what her grandfather, and later her father, thought she was better off not knowing.

"Bob and Tanya have offered to watch the children when they get here in the morning." Aida was adamant. "I will go horseback across the top. It's shorter that way and

I'm overdue to check the cows up there, anyway." She stopped midsentence, obviously irritated, "Thomas insists he should come with me—won't take no for an answer. We should be at the ruins by noon. It will be a nice little ride, and we'll get some work done at the same time."

"Fine," the professor said, "we'll set up camp today and be ready to start on the kiva tomorrow morning, early. It may take a few hours to open things up and do the initial 'in situ' photos. I would think noon should be about right."

Thomas was not quite sure why he asked Aida if he might borrow the saddle gun from the living room gun cabinet. Such venerable lever-action Winchesters had been the steady companion of horsemen in that country for over a hundred years, and still were deeply embedded in the Western psyche.

Aida opened the cabinet with the key (which is nearly always to be found on the top edge of a gun cabinet). She levered open the receiver to check that it was unloaded, then took down a box of 30-30 cartridges and passed them to Thomas. "My husband had the habit of leaving his guns loaded—it was just the two of us here and really didn't matter back then. Now, with the children, I try to see that doesn't happen."

Thomas took a handful of the rounds and handed back the box. "Can't hurt to have this along," was all he said.

Aida gave Thomas a significant glance and nodded, "I guess we might need it should a horse break a leg, or some such a business."

Both Aida and Thomas were strong riders, and in the cool morning air struck a beeline for the high ridge behind the ranch. They held their horses to a ground-eating lope for the first half mile, taking the edge off their mounts and gaining some high ground while they were fresh.

Aida and the children had just moved the cows to new pasture the week before, and she wanted to make sure their calves were doing all right in the somewhat rougher cedar breaks.

They passed through the last gate into what once had been the Buck ranch. The Buck clan had held that property since before Aida could remember, and they had been a thorn in the side of her family the entire time. The Ute family's former parcels were all part of her ranch now, and she took some satisfaction in the knowledge the former inhabitants were all either dead or had moved away. Her new holdings were finally recovering from the neglect inflicted by those previous stewards.

As they angled along the top of the ridge, Thomas pulled up to let the horses blow, and they got off to check their cinches. Aida gazed into the distance as she tightened the latigo. Far down valley she studied Hiram Buck's nephew's old trailer house. George Jim had been the craziest of the Buck family and ultimately the cause of both Hiram's and his own death. They had shot each other to death right there in that very yard.

Thomas scrutinized the decrepit trailer as well. "Do you see what I see?" he asked, shading his eyes against the midmorning glare.

"Yep." Aida flipped the stirrup down and moved the saddle horn back and forth a time or two to check the girth. "Smoke coming out of the chimney. Looks like someone's using the old place. Now who do you suppose that might be?" She didn't seem particularly concerned, and swung into the saddle in one smooth motion. "I expect we ought to drop by and see what that's about."

Thomas mounted and pushed the big paint horse ahead of Aida's roan. "Ira Buck," he murmured, and undid the tie string on his gun scabbard.

~~~~~~

Tanya Griggs was lying on the couch with her arm in a sling, watching young Caleb Begay channel surfing Aida's big, old-fashioned TV. Ida Marie lolled in the easy chair, directing her brother in the operation.

Tanya watched the children with a slowly surfacing grin. She could see Thomas Begay written all over the boy, but the girl must resemble her mother, though that was rare in her experience. Usually girls took after their fathers, and boys just as often looked more like their mothers.

Bob Mills called in from the kitchen just as the phone rang. "What does everyone want for breakfast?" He picked up the phone in the outer hall and disappeared the way he had come. When he came back, he wore an odd expression. "That was the sheriffs office. They've picked up your father but are still looking for your mother. Steven's not talking; just asked for a lawyer and clammed up. The Sheriff called to give Aida a heads up. Said Steven was apprehended alone, in Moab, at an RV park.

Tanya, wincing at the pain, came upright on the couch with a startled expression. "Poor dad. He never wanted any part of this," she cried. "It was my mother that forced him into it."

Bob moved to the couch and put an arm around her. "I know. I'm sure that will come out in time." Bob's own father was an attorney and had urged him to go into law as well. He had grown up with the law. "Perhaps he will turn state's evidence. It might keep him out of prison." He sighed. "Though I don't really see any such help for your mother."

"I don't care about my mother," Tanya snapped, "She made her decision a long time ago. I don't think our tribal elders have any idea what she's been doing." She raised her head and cast Bob a wounded glance. "I have to do something for my father."

When the children turned from the television and began taking notice of their conversation, Bob lowered his voice. Ida Marie was especially mindful of the distress in Tanya's voice. It had not been that long that she and Caleb had themselves suffered separation from their own father. The girl was still of a suspicious nature, and alert to any possible threat.

"You are in no shape to go anywhere." Bob chose his words very carefully now and spoke them in a calm and deliberate fashion, "Your father hasn't even been charged as yet. The D.A. told the Sheriff he needed more time to put everything together—probably waiting for more arrests." Bob was kind, but firm, and Tanya could see her work was cut out for her, should she intend to convince him otherwise.

"I need to go to my father," Tanya said quietly, and drew within herself, as her people sometimes do when put upon. Nonetheless, Bob could see the wheels beginning to turn. He thought he saw something in this Hopi girl, something that might eventually come in handy.

~~~~~~~~

Charlie Yazzie was not ordinarily one to feel any sort of trepidation around Anasazi ruins, but this little village in Aida's canyon was somehow different. Harley felt it too, even more in fact. Professor Custer said that was probably because these ruins had not had the spirit sucked out of them by a constant stream of tourists, pothunters, and curiosity seekers. When Charlie thought about it, he could see the truth in that. *The more accessible ruins did seem sort of 'lifeless.' This place was different, almost as though one might, at any moment, look up and see the ancients trooping back up the canyon to once again bring life to the land.* Still, the professor might be joking, and so he kept his thoughts to himself.

Harley was clearly uncomfortable, and this talk of ancients and their *chindi* did not set well with him. That was the thing about chindi, he thought, *they didn't grow old, they never went away, and even after a thousand years they might jump up and bite you on the ass.*

George Custer told Harley the Anasazi, unlike the Navajo, liked to keep their dead near them, often burying them under the floors of their houses and in abandoned rooms. This was a bit of Pueblo culture the Navajo never acquired. It was in direct contradiction to beliefs the Diné had formed over many thousands of years. In those hard times in the North, their Athabaskan forebears were a wandering people and could not always take their old and weak with them. The welfare of the many took precedence over that of the few.

This abhorrence of death might have been related to the sorrow and guilt brought about by abandoning their loved ones. The belief in *chindi,* or bad spirits, was deeply ingrained by the time they evolved into the Navajo. Some anthropologists thought these beliefs most likely developed as a mechanism to assuage sorrow and guilt. This defensive device may even have led to the custom of not speaking of the dead (or even mentioning their names). Calling a living person by his name, in his presence, might somehow identify him to a lurking *chindi.* This last, might well have been the reason for the many name changes once common among the people.

By noon the men had removed the slabs over the kiva entrance, and the bulk of the photo work had been done. George Custer thought they would wait for Aida and Thomas before he explained the significance of the findings.

Harley went down to the camp and started lunch, which in his view needn't be anything complicated. With the mandatory pot of coffee ready for the fire and sandwich makings laid out, he yelled over his shoulder for Charlie and the professor to come down and eat. As he bent to place the coffee on the grill, he suddenly straightened and looked to the scraggly line of sage above the alcove. Something had caught his eye. Just a flash, but— something. His first thought was that it might be Thomas and Aida but ruled that out after watching only a moment. They were coming horseback and would be easy to see when they broke over the horizon. And he doubted they would come in that way. It was a good distance to where they could work the horses off the rim to canyon floor. It could, of course, be just an old sardine can catching the sun exactly right.

Still, there was some little thing at the back edge of Harley's mind that didn't sit right. He slowly turned and saw Ira Buck with a rifle lying across the hood of Charlie's truck, gingerly resting the barrel on his bandaged, but useless right hand.

~~~~~~

Charlie peeked through a thin slot in the wall of the stone dwelling. The professor was just beside him, flattened against the inner wall. Both men had been hunkered down in the room, examining a potsherd of unusual design; just killing time until Thomas and Aida arrived. Charlie only looked out the little port when he heard Harley yell something about lunch. At first everything seemed as it should, but just as he glanced at his truck he saw Ira Buck's head easing up over the hood and watched, transfixed, as he slid his rifle into place. If they had still been down near the kiva he'd have been at the wrong angle to see the truck at all. He motioned to the professor to stay away from the little T-shaped doorway. Something told him Ira Buck was not alone.

Down at the camp Ira leered at Harley, "You still got my shotgun, fat boy?" He looked like he'd been holed up in a bear's den. His long, matted hair was full of little sticks and grass. The grimy bandage, soaked through with dried blood, appeared not to have been changed in days. His swollen left eye twitched and drizzled a green-tinged fluid down his cheek.

Harley glanced at the ruins but couldn't see the professor or Charlie. *Maybe they had gone into one of the little rooms behind the kiva... or maybe they...*

"Don'chu worry 'bout your friends, little man." Ira blinked to clear his vision and glanced at the ruins. "I know they're up there somewhere. They'll be back down here bye an bye—that is, if they make it this far."

Now the flash of light from the rim made sense, and Harley didn't bother to look again.

He carefully set the coffee pot on the grill and considered Ira; ignoring the question about the shotgun. "I would guess that is Ted Altman then... up there on ta rim?"

Ira's chortle turned to a hacking cough, "I would hope not." He frowned, "I shot 'im yesterday, an' when I shoot 'em they stay shot." He motioned Harley away from the fire. "That was a fancy Indian, that Ted Altman was. Talked purty too. I thought Myra might be taken in by 'im, there for awhile." His wide face turned ugly, "She wasn't though, not when she heard her daughter had been snake bit." The Ute occasionally jerked his head as though warding off a fly, but there was no fly. It was plain his hand was in a state of corruption, his forearm grotesquely swollen and discolored. The fever was on him, causing Ira to babble. Harley let him ramble on.

Ira wiped his weeping left eye on his shoulder. "That snake hadn't been meant for Myra's daughter at all. Ted Altman was supposed to leave it in George Custer's tent. But, I guess Ted Altman had his own ideas where that snake should be put."

"Now, 'bout that shotgun—my brother's gun. Our niece gimme those guns after that li'l shootout last year. You could say it's my inheritance." Ira grimaced and seemed to have trouble focusing on Harley. He moved his head forward and back, and squinted, as though to see him better. "I'd hate to lose that scattergun, these guns are about all I got left." He coughed deep in his chest, a rough, grating sound allowing Harley to think he might have a chance.

The shotgun in question was just beside the woodpile and Harley had thrown his jacket over it as he chopped firewood. It was only a few feet away, *but, of course, it doesn't take long to pull a trigger.*

"So, who *is* that up on the rim?" Harley boldly asked, "Sounds to me like you are runn'n out of people." He carefully calculated the distance to the woodpile and inched backward in that direction, hands in the air, as though frightened—which he was fast becoming.

"Don' worry yourself 'bout who's up on the rim, we got 'nough people left. Don' you worry 'bout that, little man."

~~~~~~~~

Thomas was the first one through the door of George Jim's old trailer house, rifle cocked and ready. They had watched from the corner of a pig shed long enough to believe either no one was there, or they were asleep.

Thomas thought it best they just ease up on the porch and surprise whoever might be inside. He motioned Aida back and then burst through the door. The trailer was dark and dirty, heavy with the fetid odor of rot and neglect. On top of that, there floated just a whisper of death. Toward the back bedroom, Ted Altman was tied to a chair with a neat little hole in the middle of his forehead and just a trickle of dried blood coursing down his nose.

Aida pushed her way past Thomas and, wide eyed, regarded the dead man. She remembered him from George Custer's entourage in her front yard. "I wonder what he did to end up like this?" she thought out loud. Aida was a strong woman and led a hard life in rough country. She knew death was only a heartbeat away for all living things. "I expect it don't take much to wind up dead with these people."

Thomas covered his nose and moved past the dead man, again motioning Aida back. He checked out the rear bedroom which was a filthy, airless clutter, and turned, again almost bumping into Aida, who had once more ignored him and stood staring, shaking her head at the room.

"Aida, you don't need to see all this. You should have stayed outside."

"I'm tired of people telling me what I need or don't need to see. This is my place now, and I'll see what there is to see," Aida covered her own nose as she passed back by Ted Altman.

Thomas could see Aida was rattled and trying her best not to show it. "Judging from the breakfast table in there, two, maybe three people were here. One's dead, I think since yesterday, which leaves maybe two. The stove's not even cold yet. I expect we just missed them."

Aida nodded. "Looks like they ate breakfast right in front of the dead man. It takes a certain kind of people to do that." She shook her head, held her nose, and moved toward the door. She needed some air. Outside, the two agreed whoever had been there couldn't have gone far. "I would guess we just missed them," she said echoing Thomas, which caused him to look away and raise an eyebrow.

"How far is it to the ruins, as the crow flies?" Thomas thought he knew now what was going down. There was really no other reason for these people to be out here.

"Not far, maybe an hour horseback." Aida calculated the distance by vehicle as well and knew it to be a good bit farther around, by any sort of road, "We won't be far behind going cross-country—if the horses hold out."

~~~~~~~~

Myra Griggs crouched beside a scrub oak not much taller than she, and surveyed the canyon floor through a low screen of sagebrush. She could see Ira Buck, clearly in control of the situation, but how pitiful he looked down there now. The hulking, ill-mannered Ute had always disgusted her. But even from the moment they first met she knew he would someday be useful. Even after she married Steven Griggs, Ira still doted on her, convinced they were somehow still connected, even though Myra treated him badly time after time. Her husband warned her the man was not right in the head and that she should be firmer in her rejection. He did not confront the big Ute himself, of course, as he knew that could not end well.

Myra had been a member of AFPAC since her university days and recruited Ira Buck shortly after they first met at the archaeological survey of Aida's ranch. She convinced the slow-thinking Ute he should become a part of the 'movement' and stand up for Indian rights. It was the right thing to do, she told him. He had the ability to make a real difference, she said. Ira had participated in only a few rallies and just two protests over the years, and then only at Myra's personal request.

Ira Buck *had* proven useful, and when she had called him only the month before, he had again been willing to meet with her and her friends in the Indian rights movement.

Myra looked down at the bolt-action .270 that once belonged to Ira's nephew George Jim. It had already killed two people, or so she was told. She herself was a good shot and had often hunted with her brothers. That was before the two had gone off to war and gotten themselves killed. She had actually been a better shot than either of them.

169

Certainly, she was not the equal of sharpshooter George Jim, but she was good enough.

She tried to put everything else out of her mind and remain calm. Still she seethed. Steven had run off like a yellow dog when the going got rough, and was probably back in their camper in Moab right now, fretfully awaiting her return. Their daughter, Tanya, bitten by the snake, had been the final straw for him. He had never wanted to go along with any of this. It was only her own strong will that kept him in.

Neva Travis was no better. Neva lost her nerve right after she set off the explosion. Ted Altman had placed the charge the day before and had almost been caught by Tanya. This was the trouble with white people in an Indian cause—most didn't have the courage of their convictions. She would deal with Neva, and Steven, too, when this was all over. She had thought her husband would somehow find the strength to see this thing through. She should have known better.

Myra examined her sleeve where flecks of blood had gone black in the sun, and thought *Ted Altman had made an unforgivable error in judgment when he took it upon himself to teach Tanya a lesson. He had paid the price for that mistake. If only the arrogant bastard had put the rattlesnake in George Custer's tent as planned, all might now be well. Nothing would have gone forward with the professor out of the way. Dr. Custer was not young and strong like Tanya. The snake might have been enough, and if it had not, Ted Altman had the vial of venom milked from the snake itself only days before. He could have injected it, claiming it to be anti-venom. He was, after all, the group's medic. They had picked him so carefully, too, now there are all these loose ends to tie up... and all left up to Myra Santos Griggs.*

Myra slapped at a fly and grew impatient in the increasing heat. *Am I the only one who can stay on track?*

Why am I always the one who has to hold things together? I am, after all, only second in command. That, too, might have to change. I know who is really in charge.

Pity it had taken so long to drive around by road this morning, she thought, *They might have caught everyone still in camp. They would have made easy targets then. But by the time Ira worked his way into place down below, everyone was already at work up in the ruins.*

Myra eased into position and jacked in a cartridge. She had waited long enough for the professor and Charlie Yazzie to come down for lunch. *They must have spotted Ira Buck and were afraid to show themselves.* She had told Ira to stay hidden until all three of those people were in the open. There was only one way to get them out now. She leaned into the warm stock of the rifle, took a deep breath, let it out, and squeezed the trigger ever so gently.

The fast little Spitzer boat-tail slapped Ira below the hollow in his throat, dead center of the breastbone. The light bullet blew through the bone, fragmenting with terrible internal effect. The blast still echoed as Harley Ponyboy dove for the ground and rolled for the shotgun. His first thought was that Charlie had spotted Ira and had taken him out, but he then remembered Charlie had only the .38, and such a shot would have been well beyond his range. He looked at Ira, who now wore a perplexed expression and stared down at the little well bubbling out of his shirtfront. Harley thought he saw a last pinpoint of fire in his right eye but only for an instant, and then the light went out for Ira Buck.

From the ruins, Charlie watched Ira fall, as did George Custer, now at the doorway. They exchanged glances and Charlie softly exclaimed, "Thomas got here in the nick of time." Both men started down the hill to check and make sure Harley was all right.

Myra Griggs, in the deafening after-blast of her own rifle, did not hear Thomas and Aida coming up from behind.

When they heard the shot, Thomas fell to one knee and instantly located the shooter. Myra had already worked the bolt action and raised the rifle for another shot when he yelled at her to put down the gun. Myra instantly whirled and brought her rifle to point.

The slug from Thomas's saddle gun caught her full in the chest. The 30-30 is big medicine at close range, and Myra slumped forward. Didn't even twitch.

Thomas and Aida only glanced at the obviously dead woman as they rushed past her to the rim. At the edge of the canyon they looked down on Harley, who still was not sure who had shot Ira Buck but felt lucky to be alive.

When everyone finally gathered back in the camp, it was Harley who volunteered to take the horses back to the ranch. The others would return to tell Tanya Griggs of her mother's death. Charlie had already informed authorities by way of his truck radio, and they were to meet the sheriff at Aida's ranch to give statements. Someone would have to guide authorities back to the two bodies. Everyone was relieved the danger seemed to be past—but then, things are never really what they seem.

11

The Reckoning

On the drive back to the ranch no one spoke for the first several miles, each trying to puzzle through the events of the morning. Eventually, they all came to the same conclusion; Steven Griggs, and possibly Neva Travis, were the only ones left who might have the answers they were looking for.

Charlie was the first to speak and wondered who should be the one to tell Tanya Griggs of her mother's death.

Though she did not know the girl, Aida, had at least known her mother, and said, "I'll tell her," then stared silently round the three men. "I think it needs a woman's touch."

"Fine by me," George Custer said, "Though as head of the project, and having known both women, it's rightfully my duty to tell her."

"I'll tell her, George!" Aida was adamant.

"Fine... Good," the professor said softly, looking straight ahead. "It's not like I relished the job." There was only the slightest edge to his voice.

The first thing Charlie noticed when they turned into Aida's gate were the two sheriffs cars in the yard. The second thing was that George Custer's Suburban was gone.

"I hope Tanya didn't take a turn for the worse and had to be taken back to the hospital." Aida didn't really see how this could be, as the girl appeared greatly improved when they left that morning.

As they pulled up into the yard, Thomas frowned. "Look, there's Caleb and Ida Marie in the backseat of the patrol car. Surely, Bob and Tanya didn't leave them here alone."

Charlie ground his truck to an abrupt halt, and Thomas and Aida piled out and ran to the children.

The sheriff himself was coming out of the house and came to meet Charlie, who had also stepped down from his truck. The two knew each other slightly from a law enforcement conference in Farmington. The sheriff nodded at him. "I'm not sure what's going on here, Yazzie. These kids called in right after you radioed to say you would meet us here." He removed his hat and wiped the perspiration from his brow. "They were a little hesitant to talk to us. Not been around strangers much, I guess. I figured you people would be here shortly and thought it might be best if Aida talked to them first."

Charlie pointed to Thomas, "That's their father with Aida. I'm sure they're getting the story right now."

"Well, I'll be interested to hear it. There are obvious signs of a struggle up there at the house, and it looks like someone might have left a little blood in the process. The deputy's finishing up in there." He dusted off the brim of his hat with his sleeve. "I'm not sure you know it yet, but the FBI has Steven Griggs in custody here in Cortez. Transferred him over from Moab this morning. He'd been holed up in an RV park on the river over there. The park's owner said Griggs and his wife checked in about a week ago."

Professor Custer came up and was introduced to the sheriff. "On your way in did you pass a white Suburban with state plates?" George asked.

"No, but there's two turnoffs between here and the highway. We could have missed it. Your car missing?"

"Yes. Bob Mills and Tanya Griggs did have permission to use it, though."

Thomas joined the group and nodded to the sheriff, who recognized him immediately. Thomas stuck out his hand and the sheriff took it, saying, "Long time Begay. You're not still running with Harley Ponyboy are you?"

"Not at the moment, Matt." Both of them were grinning now. "I expect he'll be sorry he missed you, though. He always said you ran the nicest jail in the county."

"What did the kids think happened here?" It had already been a long day, and the sheriff couldn't see an end in sight.

"The fact is, Matt, my kids don't know much. They took off running when the argument started and hid in the barn until everyone was gone."

"Yep, that's where my deputy found them. They said they hid out there after they made the call to 911 in the kitchen. Smart kids, for no older than they are."

George Custer interrupted, "One of my people from the university, Bob Mills, was here with Tanya Griggs to watch the children while Aida was up at the ruins today. Tanya was just released from the hospital yesterday and is still not well. We've been worried about her."

"Tanya Griggs... Oh yes, the snakebite victim search and rescue flew in, right? Her father's Steven Griggs... the FBI's holding him. From what the kids told us, you don't have to worry about the girl—it's the other person that was bleeding when they left."

Aida walked up with Ida Marie and Caleb in tow. "Hello, Matt, have you got this all figured out yet?"

"Not quite, Aida. We were hoping the children could fill us in."

"All they told us was Bob Mills and Tanya took George's truck. The kids were watching through a crack in the haymow. Caleb, here, wanted to run down and go with Tanya. Ida Marie had the good sense to hold him back. And Matt, she seemed to think Tanya had some sort of gun, at least, Ida Marie thought that's what it might be." Aida smoothed the girl's hair, and then pulled Caleb to her and gave him a big hug.

Sheriff Matt Dubois's radio crackled into life, and he walked over to tend to it. George Custer stood gazing off down the road, as though he expected to see his Suburban coming back in a cloud of dust.

Thomas whispered to Charlie, "What do you think is up with Bob and Tanya?" He looked over at the professor and caught his eye. He repeated the question, but neither the professor, nor Charlie would even venture a guess.

The professor now thought maybe they had been right when they first suspected Tanya Griggs was in league with her mother.

Charlie hesitated before saying, "I know one thing: the sheriff said he notified every agency available to set up a perimeter and called highway patrol to set up checkpoints on the main highways leading in and out of the area. But there are back roads that will get you out of here, if you know the country."

George Custer frowned, "All the area topo maps are in my truck, and Bob knows where they are. He rode with me to Aneth and followed our route into the dig using them. Said he wanted to correlate our site with the others in the area. I had them all marked on the maps. Those maps show all the back-roads. You don't think Tanya took Bob hostage, do you?"

Charlie shrugged and Thomas squinted out across the corrals. It was something neither of them could imagine.

The sheriff finished his talk on the radio, and when he came back, motioned Charlie aside. "The FBI contacted my office. Their people just picked up Neva Travis. They had an agent waiting for her when she arrived home. They are charging her with attempted murder and several other federal crimes as well. Her alliance with AFPAC is going to cost her. Several top-level people at AFPAC headquarters in Oklahoma were also picked up this morning. None of them will admit to having knowledge of what's happened out here."

After the sheriff and his deputy left, Aida took the children up to the house and got busy fixing supper—along with George Custer, who insisted on helping.

Thomas and Charlie, who had stopped to talk a moment on the veranda, saw Harley Ponyboy come riding in leading Aida's mare behind. It was nearly sundown, and the horses looked all in.

Charlie and Thomas hurried down to help with the saddles and put out some feed. They still had not had time to fill Harley in on the latest developments when Aida came out on the porch and called them in to supper. Everyone was hungry, and the men lost no time getting to the house and washed up.

Harley buttered a large dinner roll and was stuffing part of it in his mouth as Charlie told him what was going on. "Bob Mills and Tanya Griggs had some kind of a fight took George's truck and left the kids here alone. No one knows where they've gone."

Harley kept his attention on his plate, but mumbled past the mouthful of food, "I know where they are." He went on eating.

George Custer was bringing in another platter of pork chops and gave Harley a sharp look. "What do you mean, you know where they are?"

Thomas rolled his eyes and gave Charlie a look.

Harley speared a fresh pork chop off George's platter and went on eating. Harley was one of those people who could chew and talk at the same time and thought no less of himself for doing so. "You know that old abandoned farm at the end of the road on past here? Well, that's where they went. The Suburban is parked inside the hay shed. I saw it from the top of the ridge quite a ways before I turned off ta the ranch. You can't see it from the road." He looked up from his supper and smiled. "I just figured they wanted ta get away for a little 'alone time' if ya know what I mean." Harley blushed even as he said this and tried to keep his mind on his food.

Aida had followed George into the dining room and just caught the tail end of the conversation. "That's the old Johnson place. Hasn't been anyone lived there for years. That's the end of the road. There's no other way out of there." She set a bowl of mashed potatoes on the table and stood hands on hips. "Everyone figured they were trying to get away!"

Charlie was dumbstruck. "Maybe they were not trying to get away at all," he said softly. "Maybe they're smart enough to know the law will have the roads covered for a while."

Thomas whistled. "Sheriff Dubois knows it's a dead end up there, so he never even thought to look that direction. Someone's had some experience being on the run." He said this last with a hint of admiration.

"There's a good chance, then, they'll come back out after dark and make a run for it." At this point George Custer really had no idea what they might do but thought this a reasonable assumption.

Charlie agreed. "It'll be dark soon, Thomas and I might ought to take a run up there."

Aida spoke up, "Charlie, the sheriff isn't going to like that. Matt would expect you to call him."

"Aida, if we wait for the sheriff they could be long gone by the time he gets here. You can go ahead and call him after we leave. We'll consider him backup."

Harley shoved the last of his food in his mouth, "Well I'm going too. I'm the one that found 'em."

George Custer piped up as well, "That's my vehicle they've got. I should go along."

"George, someone needs to stay here with Aida and the kids. There's no telling where those people will show up next—or what they might have in mind." Charlie meant what he said, and the Professor could see he was seriously worried about Aida and the kids.

~~~~~~~

Charlie turned the lights off well before the abandoned farm and slowed the truck to a crawl. They eased along with the windows down. Listening. Thomas reached up and took the bulb out of the overhead light. When it came to arriving someplace undetected, Thomas was well tutored.

Harley said the house was off the road on the right and backed up against the ridge. When he finally pointed out the entrance, Charlie eased on past and parked the truck out of sight in the scrub oak. The three men crept silently away from the truck. They considered themselves well armed, with Charlie's .38 and Harley's shotgun, which he had grown somewhat fond of. Thomas carried the borrowed saddle gun. None of the men thought they would have to use them. A girl and a dentist shouldn't be that big a problem.

Charlie wasn't sure if they would find the missing pair in the old hayshed, or if the two runaways might have taken up shelter in the house, which was on higher ground and might provide a wider area of surveillance.

They decided to come in along the back of the hayshed and work their way around, past a broken back window to a small side door, which, when they saw it, was hanging half off its hinges. Charlie, followed closely by Thomas, crept up to the gaping door. They had Harley stay at the back corner of the shed and keep an eye on the house.

Charlie's eyes, by now, had become accustomed to the dark, and when he peered in, he could actually see quite well. The Suburban was pulled up into the shed, and he was surprised Harley could spot it even from the ridge. It would have been invisible from the road. He motioned for Thomas to cover him as he slipped in and stationed himself just inside the door. There was no outward sign of anyone in the vehicle. But when he went to its open rear window, he at once saw Tanya Griggs, bound and gagged, lying on the backseat. Her eyes were wide with fear and, upon seeing him, she shook her head violently, trying to warn him off.

As Charlie stepped up to open the rear door, someone spoke quietly from the darkness. "I thought I heard a truck go by." It was Bob Mill's voice and he sounded pretty grim. "I should have known you would figure out our little ruse." Bob moved out of the shadows, and Charlie could barely see the gun in his hand. Charlie's gun was down at his side, and Bob had the *drop* on him, as they say. "Let go the gun, Charlie, I don't want to shoot you. Truly, I don't. You're lucky it's me. Myra's the bloodthirsty one... I've had quite a time keeping her from killing people."

Charlie decided dropping the gun would be the better part of valor; it might buy him some time. Then, too, Thomas was just outside with the 30-30. Dropping the gun sounded like the right thing to do. "Okay, Bob," he said and let the Smith & Wesson fall.

Bob Mill's demeanor immediately changed for the better, friendly, almost, as he stepped forward. "If you could just kick that gun over toward me, Charlie, I'd appreciate it. And please, don't think you can rush me, or anything foolish like that. Dr. Custer may have mentioned I was a Ranger before leaving the service. I'm rather proud of that. I've kept in shape—and in practice." He looked toward the door. "Who'd you bring with you Charlie? I doubt you'd come alone. Is that Thomas out there?"

Charlie thought it best to keep quiet and let Bob do the talking.

Bob eased closer, waited, and when Charlie didn't reply, backhanded him hard enough Charlie saw stars and crashed back against the door. Charlie had heard people talk about *seeing stars* but hadn't really put much stock in it. Now he did. He shook his head and pressed a hand to his brow as though it might clear his brain of the little flashes of light. "What are you doing, Bob? Why's Tanya tied up?" They were foolish questions, he knew, but figured they might buy a little time." *Where was Thomas and what was he waiting for?*

"Oh, I don't mind you knowing, Charlie. It's not going to make much difference now, one way or the other. I let Tanya think she was forcing me to take her to town. She gave me a pretty good whack in the process, though." Bob touched the cut on his forehead. It wasn't hard to disarm her once we were up the road a bit."

"I'm doing the job you should be doing, Charlie—standing up for your peoples' rights." He bent and picked up the fallen revolver while keeping a close eye on the tribal investigator. "When Myra Griggs first called AFPAC and wanted help, we didn't think it necessary to send the number of people she requested, but when we studied the situation, we could see the Hopi might well lose a lot of ground, hard-won ground for us, Charlie, we were prominent supporters of theirs, and of the Native American Reparations Act."

The forensic dental expert and ex-army Ranger moved into the dim light of the open shed, and Charlie could see he had a fresh gash over one eye. Apparently, Tanya Griggs had put up a credible fight, considering Bob had been a Ranger and all. Charlie hoped he himself might do as well, should it come to it. *Thomas was taking his own sweet time,* there was the fleeting thought *Thomas might have gone up to the house to check it out...*

"We sent two of our very best people—me, and Ted Altman." Bob smiled. "Neva Travis was a green but she had the academic qualifications. We thought she might provide us some cover at the dig. She's not the most stable member of the group, but she's been a dedicated member of AFPAC for a long time." Bob moved back a step, "Steven Griggs was a weak link from the start, and may prove a real problem even yet. I doubt he'll hold up under FBI questioning. Myra Griggs and Ira Buck are the only stalwarts we can count on in that regard—if they can catch them. So you see, Charlie, my position is tenuous at best. I don't have a whole lot to lose at this point."

Charlie thought this might be the time to play his trump card. "I'm afraid it may be worse than you know, Bob. Myra Griggs is dead, along with Ira Buck and Ted Altman. Neva Travis is in the hands of the FBI. I wouldn't count on her holding up under questioning any better than Steven Griggs. I expect it will be more of a race to see who's first to accept immunity and turn state's evidence." Charlie thought he saw Bob Mills flinch at this news and went on, "There's still time for you to save yourself, Bob. Only you know the higher-ups in the 'movement.' The FBI has had their eye on AFPAC for a long time. I'm almost certain you could cut a deal."

"No, I couldn't do that. My father and brother both are members—both lawyers. There are a lot of whites with us Charlie. Academics mostly, lefties, many of them. I couldn't do that to them." He looked away for a moment. "No, unless I get away clean, I'm done." Bob smiled a sad little smile, "But that doesn't surprise you, does it, Charlie?"

"What about Tanya, Bob? I thought she meant something to you?"

"She did, Charlie. She was the only leverage I had over Myra Griggs. That's why I stuck close to her. I knew when Ted Altman screwed up with the rattler that Myra would kill him first chance she got. She and Tanya may not have thought alike on a lot of things, but blood is blood among the Hopi." Bob shifted his gun to the other hand and shoved Charlie's .38 into his hip pocket. "No, Ted was actually the one who had feelings for Tanya, and when she rejected him and his offer to join us, he lost it. I was in the service with him. Not only was he a first-class medic but one of the best explosives men in the business. We had to fake his academic resume, of course, but he was the real deal otherwise. He just let his feelings get away with him is all."

Charlie closed his eyes and hoped Tanya Griggs couldn't hear this conversation. For one thing, it would be a rough way to find out about her mother.

Bob abruptly stuck his gun in Charlie's face and shouted toward the door, "Thomas! You'd better get in here if you want to see your friend get through this alive." He waited. "I'm serious, Thomas. I'll give you to the count of three... One..."

A calm voice from behind said, "Bob, you better put that gun down right now." Harley was leaning in the back window of the shed and had his 12 gauge pump leveled at Bob's back. "I'll do it, Bob. Just drop the gun."

"Harley is that you?"

"It's me, Bob, and I'm going ta shoot you if you don' drop that gun." Harley was nearly invisible in the black hole of the window. His voice turned hollow and cold. "This is a 12 gauge... with double-ought buckshot. No one walks away from one of these, Bob." Harley leaned in a little closer and his voice raised just an octave. "Don' turn around with that gun in your hand." Harley's intentions were deadly clear.

Bob acted as though he didn't quite understand and slowly turned toward the sound of Harley's voice. That's when Charlie coldcocked him with such force both men went down—just barely under the blast of Harley's shotgun. Bob's pistol went flying and Charlie scooped it up, then retrieved his own .38 from the hip pocket of the unconscious dentist.

Thomas half-staggered through the sagging door, nose gushing blood. He covered the prone Bob Mills with the 30-30. "You all right, college boy?"

"Your timing needs work."

"My 'timing' was okay until Bob slammed you into that door I was coming through." He reached and tweaked his battered nose back into line. "Nose is broken—again." He winced, but continued to manipulate the nose into some semblance of its former self. "Not to mention, that load of buckshot nearly took my head off."

Harley Ponyboy, unperturbed, looked on with interest. "One of you boys should let Tanya loose" was his only comment.

The sound of sirens wailing in the distance caused Charlie to cock his head. "The sheriff will be happy to see he doesn't have another body to haul off. And so am I."

12

The Mystery

When all was said and done, three people were dead and three in jail. Steven Griggs was the lucky one, being first to accept immunity. Neva Travis, due to her ongoing cooperation, also was accorded prosecutor's "special consideration." She would go to prison, but the length of her sentence could vary considerably. The FBI felt they were on the verge of a major incursion into the affairs of AFPAC and were determined to put together a strong case whatever it might take. Already several additional arrests had taken place in Oklahoma. Bob Mills, was charged equally with the others. Things did not look good for Bob Mills.

Aida invited Tanya Griggs to continue her recuperation at the ranch. The girl's left arm was still somewhat weak and might always be, according to the doctors. Her father had been whisked away to a government "witness protection" program, and with her mother gone as well, she had nowhere else to go until her classes at ASU resumed. While still in a considerable state of grief and denial, she was yet determined to rejoin the project and see things through.

George Custer, for his part, had learned his lesson and was now determined not to hurry this new investigation. He and Harley continued work at the new dig and already had sent numerous samples and bone fragments to be examined at the university lab. Harley was in awe of the learned professor and made an attentive and capable assistant. Dr.

Custer, having sprung from common stock himself, had a way with such people.

Charlie and Thomas went home for a short time before returning for the final interpretation of findings in the kiva. Both men had found everything at home being managed in a calm and efficient manner and were somewhat at a loss to see things going so well without them.

Charlie's infant son appeared well rested and was beginning to take a real interest in the world. Aunt Annie and Clyde were still there, of course, and seemed to have things well in hand. Sue assured him that his spending another few days at the dig would be fine with her. She was getting a pretty good handle on motherhood. She said privately it might even be time for her helpers to go home. Charlie asked her to let them stay on, just until he returned. She could see it would ease his mind and agreed to wait till he got back so *he* could handle the dismissal of Aunt Annie and Clyde.

Professor Custer's team was eager to see how strong the correlation was between his soon-to-be-published paper and the actual findings at the dig. It was Charlie's considered opinion the paper might stir up even greater controversy among Dr. Custer's colleagues, possibly even compromise his position at the university.

Charlie went so far as to urge his former mentor to exercise caution. "George, have you considered the effect on your job should your detractors petition the university? Tenure is tenure but it only goes so far." *The University must have limits regarding what they were willing to support in the Professor's unorthodox theories.*

"Not really, Charlie. I won't let the threat of personal consequences interfere with my pursuit of truth in science."

Charlie thought this a dangerous stance considering George's known proclivity for bizarre conclusions.

The professor stood firm in the conviction that his years of research would bear him out. He remained resolute in his determination to go forward with the publication of his work "come hell or high water," as he put it. He just wanted this one last bit of evidence.

~~~~~~~

Charlie and Thomas were in the lead vehicle, followed by Aida, Tanya, and the kids. Aida and Thomas had agreed the children might be allowed along but were not to go into the kiva itself. The children would be going back home with Thomas soon, and Aida was determined to be with them as much as possible. Also, Charlie thought he had seen a definite thaw in the relations between Aida and the Professor, though what might come of that he did not know.

Thomas rolled down the truck's passenger-side window. It was early and still cool with just a chance of rain promised for the afternoon. "Well, it's a hell of a thing how this all turned out. Who'd a thought the 'movement' could infiltrate a university research team with three people, and have another three working on the outside?"

"AFPAC was determined, that's for sure. It will be interesting to see how it all shakes out when the trial starts. But I'm thinking it's about all over for AFPAC"

"I still can't believe Bob Mills was the big dog... you'd of thought it would be an Indian."

Charlie smiled, "Well, Ted Altman was a Cherokee. Myra Griggs a Hopi, and Ira Buck a Ute. Seems like the Indians were pretty well represented."

"Do you think many Dinè are members of AFPAC?"

"I expect there are some—young people mostly. I know there were at UNM. I think it's important for the Navajo Nation to be represented in the legitimate 'Indian movements' but these extreme splinter groups that are popping up around the country don't do anyone any good."

"The question is; how do people know what they're getting into until it's too late?"

Charlie just shook his head and eased the truck down into the wash leading to the ruins.

Thomas looked to the horizon in the direction of the former Buck ranch. He was still uneasy about the Bucks, especially when his children were at Aida's. Secretly, he hoped she and the professor would mend their fences and get back together, for everyone's sake. "I hope this is the last we hear from those Buck's. There doesn't seem to be any end of them."

"Well, you would think it's the end, but then, we've thought that before." Privately, Charlie thought, *I doubt what is left of the Buck clan will pose a problem for Aida, or anyone else.*

When they pulled into camp, the professor and Harley were taking their midmorning break. Smiling, the pair went to meet the vehicles and laughed when the children immediately headed to the little stream and proceeded to splash each other with the cold water. Caleb grabbed a stick and began turning over stones to see what he could find. Many turned out to be broken pottery shards scattered across the streambed—some from vessels dropped by children (who were much like him) sent to fetch water eons ago. Ida Marie kept a close eye on her brother. He was quick as a chipmunk and just as prone to getting into things he shouldn't.

The professor greeted Aida with a grin and she smiled in return. He was happy to see Tanya, too. No one spoke of the earlier shootout, and the girl didn't ask but was subdued and thoughtful. Aida brought forth a large picnic basket, and Thomas unloaded a cooler of cold drinks. The sun was still blocked by the canyon wall, making it shady and cool in the camp. Aida felt they should have lunch before going up to the ruins. *Some might not have the belly for food afterwards*, she thought to herself.

Aida, with Tanya and the children's help, had outdone herself. There was fried chicken, potato salad, and baked beans, set off by two chocolate cakes made from scratch. Harley's cooking had already worn thin, and George Custer was ready for a change. The children were called in and lunch was served.

Charlie stood looking up to the ruins. *What would these ancient people have thought to see such goings on in front of their old home?*

Harley passed him a plate and he filled it and went to sit by Thomas on the tailgate of the truck. He gestured up to the kiva and said, "If only those little people could have been locked in time, hidden away here for eternity," and immediately felt foolish for saying it.

Thomas slowly finished chewing his mouthful and grew unusually pensive as he said, "Well in a way, I guess you could say that is exactly what has happened."

Charlie, knowing the future of these people, nodded his head. "It's hard to imagine what terror stalked this land in those end times. People starving and watching their children starve too, then finally making the desperate decision to leave and find someplace less affected by the drought." He looked down at the ground. "Usually, the decision came too late I guess. Bands of their own kind from the smaller outlying settlements were probably the first to run out of food. And they began to prey on the larger settlements—those with the more favorable locations and larger reserves. The migration probably happened gradually, clan by clan, leaving those left behind unable to defend themselves against the marauders. A number of area sites show the deadly effect of the intruders' attacks and the cannibalistic aftermath—true signs of war, with human remains showing broken skulls and others injuries from arrows, stone axes, and knives, then... the unmistakable signs of the butchering."

When the picnic was over and everything put away Tanya took the children back down to the water, saying she would go up to the kiva later, alone. "Those are my people up there... no matter what." Looking away to the rim of the canyon, she whispered, "I will go alone to say my goodbyes."

The rest of the group trudged up the hill and one by one entered the kiva. The sun was at the right angle to cast a muted light through the chamber's opening. They could see the built-in stone bench around the interior, seating for now-forgotten ceremonies. Several cross beams had been freshly shored up with poles, but everything else was just as it had been for over a thousand years. Their boots raised little poofs of dust and a gentle haze filtered down from the cedar bark and pole roof.

Harley and the professor had carefully brushed away the accumulation of sand and dust and once again the remains of these last few residents were exposed to the filtered light of day.

Aida took a deep breath and let it out with an audible sigh. *All these years, I've waited to see this. Now I understand. George was right. I will never think of this place in the same way again.*

Dr. George Custer stood in the center of the dimly lit chamber and began his account—what he felt certain had taken place in the end times of the great migration. "There has been much evidence over the years supporting cannibalism in the final days of these people. A number of proven instances are found just miles from here. Among knowledgeable scientific investigators, incidents of cannibalism are no longer disputed."

The professor grew even more serious as he looked around the circle. "What I'm about to tell you is not as widely believed, though it is just as well supported by scientific evidence." An almost palpable pall fell over the chamber as the professor went on with his talk. "Theories have varied widely as to the cause of these aberrations. Most thought they followed sporadic instances of war during desperate times, with the victors eating the vanquished. But you must keep in mind that Aztec beliefs and rituals had been trickling up from Mexico for years, and the *Kachina* culture may have already gained a foothold across this area. Sacrifice was probably not unknown. The fact that this particular incident took place in a kiva, by itself, indicates something ceremonial in nature." And here the Professor lowered his voice. "The skeletal remains you see laid out here beside the fire pits are different. First, they are only of the very young and very old. These were the age groups most often left behind in many primitive cultures. Leaders knew there was little chance of them surviving a hard journey with limited food and shelter. Food stocks, by this time, were most probably already depleted, and the people teetered on the edge of starvation.

"The human remains you see in this kiva do not show the usual signs of death suffered in violent attacks. These people might have been strangled, or somehow suffocated. It's hard to say at this point. They were then systematically dismembered, the bones sometimes defleshed. The typical marks of flint knife on bone are unmistakable—the same pattern found in large game kills when butchered for food. Some pieces had been stewed, judging from the white bleached bones, and others roasted over the fire—indicated by the burned bone ends." The professor gazed thoughtfully at the bones. "There had been only one way to take these people with them, and in the process gain strength for the journey, possibly even satisfy the new *Kachina* Gods."

The professor paused for effect. "Given the time and situation there is a certain logic to their thinking, especially when one considers the incoming Aztec beliefs being embraced by these people." Now the professor singled out the three Dinè in the group. "I believe Charlie will agree there's good evidence his Athabaskan forbearers often made these same decisions in the far North and continued to do so into latter times. Indeed, many prehistoric people followed much the same course."

The group remained silent, mesmerized by the professor's interpretation, the spell finally broken by the distant roll of thunder.

When they returned to camp, Tanya was also just returning from a short hike with the children. She could tell by the edgy expressions that for most it had been a disquieting experience.

The professor knew Tanya was well aware of his views on the contents of this and certain other sites in the area. She had known of his work for some time, mostly from her mother, Myra Griggs. "Tanya, are you sure you want to go up there?"

Aida, too, came forward and took the girl's hands. "Tanya, perhaps it would be better if you did this later, when you are more up to it."

"No, Aida, like you, I have waited a long time to decide for myself what happened up there. It's time to see whether or not my mother was right." She looked up at the rim above the ruins. "I need to know it now more than ever."

"I could go with you, if you like." Charlie somehow knew the girl would decline, but thought it only right that he ask.

Harley brought her a flashlight. "It's pretty dark in there now. Watch your step going down the ladder."

As everyone watched the young Hopi woman climb the path to the kiva, Thomas, spoke for the first time. "I hope this brings her some kind of peace, but I don't really see how it can."

The men fell to breaking camp as George Custer now considered himself finished with this phase of the investigation. The lab results would not be in for several days, and while he was certain of the outcome, he needed official verification for his paper.

It was coming on evening when the onerous job of loading the trucks was finished. The children, too, were worn out by the day's activities and knew it was time to go. Thomas wanted to return to the ranch and begin packing for their trip home. It was finally decided that Aida and Thomas would take the children on ahead. Charlie and the Professor, along with Harley, would wait for Tanya to come down, and then close up the kiva before the four of them returned to the ranch.

As it grew later, the professor noted it would soon be dark, and they really should make the drive out in daylight. He was just about to send Harley up to hurry Tanya along when they heard the muffled gunshot from the ceremonial chamber. The three men exchanged startled glances but knew instantly what had come to pass—and grew sick at heart even as they rushed toward the kiva. Once again the great mystery of the Anasazi had touched beyond the brooding curtain of time to claim yet another of their own.

The end

ABOUT THE AUTHOR

Writer, poet R. Allen Chappell's work has appeared in magazines, literary and poetry publications, and has been featured on public radio and television. He grew up in New Mexico, at the edge of the great reservation.

Navajo Autumn is the precursor to his Navajo Nation mystery series.
Boy Made of Dawn is the second stand-alone novel in the trilogy.
Ancient Blood is the third and latest story in the series.

His unrelated short story collection *Fat of The Land* is also out on Amazon in both paperback and Kindle.

He and his wife spend most winters Mexico and summers at home in Colorado, where he pursues a lifelong interest in the pre-history of the region. He welcomes reader comments at: rachappell@yahoo.com

If you've enjoyed this book, please consider going to its Amazon book page to leave a short review. It would be most appreciated.

Glossary

1. Acheii — Grandfather *
2. Anasazi — Pueblo ancestors
3. Athabaskan — Navajo rootstock *
4. Ashkii Ana'dlohi — Laughing boy
5. A-hah-la'nih — affectionate greeting*
6. Ah-wayh — Baby
7. Chindi — (or chinde) Spirit of the dead *
8. Chih keh — young woman
9. Chosovi — blue bird (Hopi)
10. Dinè — Navajo people
11. Dinè Bikeyah — Navajo country
12. Hataalii — Shaman (Singer)*
13. Hastiin — (Hosteen) Man or Mr. *
14. Hogan — (Hoogahn) Traditional dwelling
15. Hozo — To walk in beauty *
16. Kachina — deities
17. Shih-chai — Father *
18. Tsé Bii' Ndzisgaii — Monument Valley
19. Yaa' eh t'eeh — Greeting; Hello
20. Yeenaaldiooshii — Skinwalker; witch*

See Notes *

Notes

1. *Acheii — Grandfather – there are several words for Grandfather depending on how formal the intent and the gender of the speaker.

2. *Athabaskan — The Northern Paleo-Indian ancestors, of the Navajo and Apache. Sometimes referred to as Athabasca.

4. *A-hah-la'nih — A greeting - affectionate version of Yaa eh t'eeh, generally only used among family and close friends.

6. *Chindi – When a person dies inside a hogan, it is said that his chindi or spirit remains there forever, causing the hogan to be abandoned. Chindi are not considered benevolent entities. For the traditional Navajo, just speaking a dead person's name may call up his chindi and cause harm to the speaker.

11. *Hataalii – Generally known as a "Singer" among the Dinè, these men are considered "Holy Men" and have apprenticed to older practitioners—sometimes for many years—to learn the ceremonies. They make the sand paintings that are an integral part of the healing and know the many songs that must be sung in the correct order.

12. *Hastiin — Literal translation is "man" but is often considered the word for "Mr." as well. Hosteen is the usual Anglo version.

14. *Hozo – For the Navajo "hozo" (sometimes hozoji) is a general state of well-being, both physical and spiritual, that indicates a certain "state of grace," which is referred to as "walking in beauty." Illness or depression, is the usual cause of "loss of hozo," which puts one out of sync with the people as a whole. There are ceremonies to restore hozo and return the ailing person to a oneness with his people.

17. *Shih-chai — Father. There are several words for Father depending on the degree of formality intended and sometimes even the gender of the speaker.

18. *Yeenaaldiooshii – These witches, as they are often referred to, are the chief source of evil or fear in the traditional Navajo superstitions. They are thought to be capable of many unnatural acts, such as flying, or turning themselves into werewolves and other ethereal creatures; hence the term Skinwalkers, referring to their ability to change forms or skins.

Ancient Blood

Made in the USA
Las Vegas, NV
22 December 2020